Mordec and the Lost Boys

THE THRILLING ADVENTURES OF MORDEC THE VIKING

Mordec Raids England
Mordec's Quest
Mordec and the Hidden Hand
Mordec and the Lost Boys
Mordec the Conqueror

THE THRILLING ADVENTURES OF
MORDEC THE VIKING

BOOK 4

Mordec and the Lost Boys

JILLIAN BECKER

Typesetting and Cover Design by
FormattingExperts.com

Published by Gothenburg Books
ISBN 978-1-7327275-6-4

contents

Mordec and the Lost Boys

To my grandchildren:
Matthew & Aaron Slipper
Jessica & Elizabeth Dilworth
Sam & Charlotte Westrop

delivered by magic

On one night of the year and one night only, when the last of the harvest was in and the moon at its full, Zarath of the East put his magic at the service of the lords and folk, and granted one wish—'One wish *only*,' he emphasized—to anybody, high or low.

The wish had to be serious; what Zarath called 'a heartfelt need'. Nothing frivolous. Nothing absurd. No wanting to be changed into something else, a beast or fish or insect or everlasting golden bird—'Because,' he said, 'there is a Sacred Ban on changing you back again, and I wouldn't want you to do something you'll regret!' No asking for doom to be called down on a neighbour. The old could not become young again, or a child instantly grow up. No riches pouring from the sky or fountaining from the earth.

But something lost could be found, something wrong could be righted, something missing could be supplied, something forgotten could be recalled. If a wish was judged by Zarath to be unworthy he wouldn't accept it. An acceptance of a wish was as good as a promise to grant it.

Lately he'd begun to feel that his magic wasn't being found as impressive as it used to be. He was getting on in years, had grey in his hair, and feared that as his youthful energy and inventiveness diminished, his tricks would become too repetitive: fire that burnt nothing, water that left nothing wet. His general usefulness was not questioned. He did his routine job of making the (very fertile) soil of Runnydale continue to be fertile; the (plentiful) rains fall plentifully. But he had determined that he simply must come up with something really spectacular and utterly amazing on the Night of the Granting this year. And—because luck had favored him—he would!

Tonight was the night. Folk from near and far were bringing their wishes to the great hall of Runnydale, where the Ceremony of the Hearing took place; and others, the greater number, who had no wishes likely to be granted but good appetites for the feast provided free of charge by the Rulers after the Ceremony was over, gathered on the wide lawns in front of the hall.

Zarath had no view of the front lawns from his tower on a far corner of the palace. But he knew that wish-bearers and their witnesses, old and young, had started arriving since early morning, and that the numbers on the roads had grown through the afternoon. It had been a lovely bright day after alternating squalls and drizzles of rain for hours in the morning had made everybody anxious that the outdoor feast, with suckling pigs turning on spits and open barrels of ale, would have to be canceled, allowing only those who had been granted a place in the great hall—so as to bring their wishes to Zarath—would be able to attend. But the sun had smiled, and given way to a full moon now rising in a cloudless sky.

The gates would be open, and the folk jostling on the paths of the palace grounds and settling on the lawns, to await the thrilling sound of the trumpets that would launch the Ceremony.

Zarath was impatient to begin, being sure he would excel himself tonight. Throughout the day, secluded in his chamber for most of the time, he could feel his powers rising within him like the autumn tide of the grey sea that washed the rocky shores of Runnydale.

As the set hour drew near, he put on long white robes over the woolly vest he wore almost all year round in this damp north-western climate. He crowned his thick black hair, which hung to his shoulders in oiled ringlets, with a bronze circlet of thirteen spikes, twelve bearing each a sign of the zodiac, and the one on the forehead a golden sun. Along the waves of his black square-cut wrinkly beard and on his eyebrows he stuck chips of precious stones with gum from Araby. He reddened his lips with the juice of mulberries. On his feet he strapped ivory pattens which raised him several inches, making him seem impossibly tall. Finally he perfumed his hands with a paste of jasmine crushed in precious asafoetida, a jar of which, sealed with wax, he kept in a square silver box whose handle was a fat scaly silver dragon, its roaring-open mouth studded with tiny real milk teeth fallen from the gums of weaned monkeys.

All this, his look, his scent, helped to make Zarath feel extraordinary, an object of wonder. And as long as he inspired wonder he could never be denounced, destroyed, or chased away. Or so he trusted and hoped. He believed his powers were valued and esteemed in this far Western land where he had settled seven years ago. He was still a mysterious stranger to the people, and as such he meant to remain. None knew where he came from. Many said his home was far in the East: Persia or India, perhaps. And he didn't contradict them. Some said he was the greatest magician in the world, and he didn't contradict *them* either.

Zarath went to his window. The moon was out, big, round and glowing as a polished brass trumpet. He saw the last of the visitors, stragglers, hurrying along the paths, past the gardens, disappearing from his view among the trees of the orchard as they moved towards the chalk-white road leading to the gates of Runnydale Court on the other side of the palace. It seemed to him that there were even more of them than last year.

He was right. The crowd was dense, and loud was the noise of their chatter.

The trumpets sounded. Suddenly, dramatically, their brilliant summons blazed out across the meadows and the town, twelve times. A thousand settled birds were startled into rising with a rustle like a rainburst, and peacocks in the gardens of the palace were set screaming. But the folk fell silent. Those who were moving about stopped and froze stock-still. A thrill flowed slow and sharp as honey through them, body and soul. The long deep reverberation of the twelfth stroke travelled on, fading at last into a seemingly inextinguishable quiver of the evening air.

Every grown-up who had registered his or her name for entry to the Ceremony was handed a lighted candle by a yellow-liveried palace servant at the entrance to the hall. There more servants waved them into orderly rows. Row on row, the candle-flames fluttered in trembling hands, and by breaths quickened with excitement. When all were in and the sound of shuffling feet stopped, and as much quiet prevailed as could be expected where some hundreds of impatient people were gathered, a harp rippled, and he, the famous Zarath of the East, materialised before them like an unearthly messenger from Beyond.

He seemed to grow from the floor of the platform at the end of the hall. There he stood with his face underlit by a row of lanterns at his feet. He towered, he bowed, he glittered, he smiled. His teeth were wonderfully white. Awed, the audience caught its breath in a gasp and let it out on a sigh, all together, as though it was a single creature. The harp music faded away as Zarath stretched out his arms, opened them wide, and spoke with an impressive rolling of Rs.

'Grrreetings! I am Zarrrath, come from afar, but rrresiding among you these many years. Your humble servant.'

He bowed very low, sweeping his right arm from across his body and stretching it up to point to the raftered roof, and held it so as he straightened.

'Frrriends! Make the rrrafters rrring with your cheers for our grrreat Rrrulers, the Lord Alger and the Lord Humfrrrey.'

And cheer they did. 'Hurrah! Hurrah!'

Zarath snatched a white wand out of the air. The sudden gesture, the mysterious appearance of the thing, stopped the cheering abruptly.

Zarath tapped the floor of the platform, and water rushed across it, a sudden flood, from side to side, and disappeared, leaving the boards as dry as if they had never been wetted at all.

Zarath turned his back on the watchers. There was the sound of wind, the folds of his long cloak stirred, it bellowed out, flapped as though caught in a gale, fell back into place and all was still.

Zarath turned to face them again, waved his wand jerkily over the platform, and spurts of fire licked up, now here, now there. He tapped the floor with the wand and the flames were instantly gone.

All this was done in silence. The audience watched silently, solemnly. He had entertained them with water and fire before, but it was always an awesome sight.

Now he strode to the side of the platform, flung his wand down, and lo! It turned into a squirming yellow snake. Women screamed. He snatched it up by its tail, and it was a wand again. They had never seen him do that before.

'Again, again!' some voices cried. The magician complied. Down went the wand, there the snake writhed, but seized by its tail it was a wand again.

Now the invisible harp played as Zarath moved to seat himself on the cushions of an elaborately carved and gilded throne-like chair placed centre-stage. He settled himself, arranged his robes, and the music stopped. The hall was hushed. The magician swished his wand once from side to side, then held it out rigidly towards the audience. He invited them in ringing tones: 'Come, my friends, come and whisper your wishes to me.'

The first petitioner climbed six steps, stood whispering before the great magician, and went on his way, descending another flight of steps on the other side of the platform. He was followed by the rest: men, women and children one by one climbed the steps, approached the magician, whispered, and returned to their places. Leaning a little forward to hear their wishes, Zarath held a small brass shield to protect his beard from the candles. It reflected their flickering light. Beyond it his face was in shadow. To most of them he responded with a regretful shake of the head. Sadly, his face indicated, that and that and that could not be done. Most of them were, as usual, bringing him the wrong sort of wishes. But every now and then he nodded, moved the shield aside, smiled his frost-white smile, and murmured 'Within a week from now you will find it', or that so many days from to-morrow a something 'will be returned', or 'will be healed', or 'will have been mended', or 'will have gone away'.

For these trusting folk, fulfillment, when granted, was always postponed. But for the lords it was different. After the many had asked and a few among them had received promises, the turn of the lords came. They sat well apart from each other in the minstrel gallery high at the back of the hall, with uniformed guards and liveried attendants standing behind them, and were not accorded the privilege of secrecy. They must ask for what they desired aloud for all to hear.

Every year the two Lords of Runnydale—a pair of cousins in perpetual dispute with each other—would rise and speak one at a time in alphabetical order; first Alger the Soft, then Humfrey the Hard.

Alger the Soft—a chubby, pale-haired, freckled person—had, at his first go when Zarath of the East had newly arrived a few years back, asked for 'Humfrey's heart to be softened', only to be told by Zarath that it couldn't be done. Since then, Alger had expressed simple wishes, such as to be served better by the Runners; to have salad more often; to win at this game or that (which he'd play against Zarath himself after dinner on Sundays). These modest desires had been gratified. So on Nights of the Granting he'd always start off by thanking Zarath in high-pitched ringing tones for whatever he'd magicked for him during the past year. This was at Zarath's own suggestion, to let the crowd know that Alger was a satisfied customer.

Tonight he called out his polite requests: for a good harvest, someone who could read his letters to him without stammering, and to be better at chess.

'All shall be granted, my lord,' Zarath called back.

Humfrey rose to his feet. Tall, thin, dark-complexioned, black-eyebrowed, he was in every way different from his cousin. Year after year he would ask for the same thing, never mind how often he was told he couldn't have it. The crowd expected to hear it asked for again tonight and they were not disappointed.

In a growling tone not far from anger, he declared: 'As you are perfectly aware, there's only one thing I want. You've known it for ages but I'm still waiting. How many years have I been asking? Five? Six? I'm a patient man, but this is getting more than a little bit irksome. Eh? In case you've forgotten it—Have you forgotten it? You shake your head but let me remind you—*I want him out.*' Everyone knew he meant Alger, but still he pointed at him. 'He gets in my *hair.*' Dramatically, Humfrey pushed his fingers through his upstanding black hair, seized two clumps of it and pretended to be trying to pull it out. 'I want him gone, one way or another, dead or alive. Right? You understand? You've got it? It's not really hard to grasp is it? And excuse *me* but I thought I heard you say you're a magician. Or did I hear wrong? No? Yes? You *are* a magician? You can make wishes come true? Very well then. That's my wish. You've heard it. Now please, *please*, do what I ask. It isn't much. Just *make him vanish*! I don't mind where to. Spain. Baghdad. Constantinople. The moon. Anywhere but *here.*'

As usual at this point he covered his face with his hands as if in despair and sat down.

'Sorry, my lord, but it can't be done,' Zarath called back politely and regretfully. 'I'm really sorry, but it's just not possible.'

The harp music played sadly for a few moments.

Next, usually, was the Orphan. He sat on a low stool between the carved chairs of the Lords of

Runnydale, a boy not yet eight years old who had been at Runnydale since he was three. His wish would provide the climax and conclusion of the evening. It was always for some toy, and Zarath would make some passes in the air, mumble something, and the object of desire would appear in his hand. This instant magic always went down well with the crowd. They would laugh, break into a buzz of wondering and appreciative chatter, and applaud Zarath as he made his farewell bow and, smiling his white smile, disappear.

But this year, Zarath had been forewarned, a newcomer would be tending a wish before the Orphan: a princess from the East, a very large lady with an eye-catching ginger moustache that Alger rather envied. She was seated beside him. She did not rise when Zarath pointed his wand at her and smiled. She addressed him in a language no one in the crowd could even name, let alone understand. She spoke with much feeling, and now and then Zarath nodded as he listened. So he knew this outlandish lingo!

He heard her out and said in English so everyone could hear and understand him: 'Madam, your wish must be heard by all these people in order for me to grant it. It must be spoken by you yourself. I therefore urge you to repeat yourself in words that all may understand.'

The lady spoke again, even more feelingly, in the same language as before. This time Zarath shook his head. She clicked her tongue indignantly, but stopped speaking.

'Next please,' Zarath said crisply, and the little orphan boy rose, hurried to the spiral stairs at the back of the gallery and came down into the hall, The candle-holders made a way for him to pass, and he trotted to the platform, smiling and eager. His light brown hair shone under the lantern light. The magician stood waiting for him at the top of the six steps leading up to the platform, and when he came within reach Zarath lifted him, carried him to the throne-like chair, and stood him on the cushions. Though he stood there upright, holding on to the chair's carved back to steady himself, Zarath had still to bend a little towards him so that the boy could whisper in his ear. The crowd waited. It seemed a long wish.

'What's he asking for?' a young man had the temerity to sing out.

'Yeah' said another, 'we want to know what he's saying.'

'C'mon,' said a third, 'you always let us know what he's wishing for.'

Zarath quietly conversed with the boy for a few moments more, looking into his green eyes, then turned to the crowd and said, 'The Orphan will tell you what he wishes for. Go on, dear boy, tell them what it is.'

'You see,' the boy said, not shyly, but in a happy voice easily heard, 'I'm a Viking, and somehow I lost my parents and they went away without me, and, well, it's nice here, everyone looks after me and everything, and there are lots of other children to play with, but I really want another Viking boy. A bit older than me. To teach me things. That's what I've asked Zarath for this time. And you'll give him to me, won't you, Zarath?'

'So what you want is a Viking for a friend? A boy bigger than you, right? That's what you really and truly want?'

'Yes, please, Zarath,' the Orphan affirmed in an eager, trusting tone, his eyes bright with anticipation, his hands—or rather his fingertips—clapping together.

'How old should he be? How much older than you?'

'I'm eight so he should be at least twelve,' the boy said.

'Fourteen, fifteen?' Zarath suggested.

The boy nodded.

'Very well then,' Zarath said. 'It's a difficult wish to grant, I must tell you that. But I'll try specially hard, and granted it shall be.'

Leaving the boy standing on the chair, the magician went to the wall at the back of the platform, and lifted down a long leather and bronze shield from its hook. He lowered it to the floor and held on to it with one hand. It was more than half his own impressive height. Closing his eyes and tilting back his head, he loudly and rhythmically intoned this spell:

Powers of air and powers of fire,
make a Viking boy suspire.
He should be fifteen years old,
strong and brave and wise and bold.

No sooner was the last word spoken than the mysterious wind was heard to blow, this time loud as a tempest: flames licked up from the ground round the shield, only to be put out seconds later by a rush of water which swirled over them and drained fast away. Zarath turned his back to the audience and facing the shield took hold of it with both hands. After a moment of suspense he snatched up the shield and stepped aside. A heap of sea-sand was revealed and on it a body, bare footed, clothed in a ragged blue garment, was lying very still.

No one in the crowd or up in the gallery made the least sound. The Orphan stared at the body with his mouth open. It was as if no one could believe what he saw with his own eyes.

'Awake!' Zarath commanded.

Harp music rippled, and the body stirred.

'Arise!' said the magician.

The music rippled more thrillingly, and the person sat up: a fair-haired boy, about fifteen years old. He looked round helplessly, seeming not to know where he was. He blinked as though the lights dazzled him, then, becoming aware that there were people looking at him, he stood up and a little unsteadily half-stepped, half-jumped off the sand-pile, reaching out with both hands for something steady to hold on to. Zarath took the hands in his and drew the boy to the centre of the platform where the Orphan stood on the chair, and stationed him there with his back to the hall full of silent, breathless, astonished watchers.

The boy stood blinking at the Orphan, then at Zarath, and then looked round at the rows of faces. Cheers broke out from the gallery, followed by louder cheers and wild applause from the hall. Some of the women in the crowd were so overcome that they laughed and wept and clapped at the same time. The strange boy bowed his head, keeping hold of an arm of the chair with both hands.

'Well done, Zarath, well done,' Alger shouted shrilly from the gallery.

Zarath beamed and bowed in all directions, raised his hands to the gallery, bowed again, very low. He felt a strong sense of relief. He'd brought it off. He'd surpassed himself. Could they doubt now that he was worthy of his post?

'Zarath! Zarath!' numerous voices cried, rising one above another to acclaim the master of magic. The harp music was quite drowned out. The invisible harpist struck a final chord and gave up playing.

When the cheering died down enough for him to be heard, Zarath declared to the Orphan, 'Here is the friend you wished for. Ask him his name. Tell him yours.'

The little boy stooped to look under the bowed head of the big boy. 'My name is Leif,' he said, 'and you are my Wish-Come-True.'

With both hands he tried to lift his Wish-Come-True's head. The big boy lifted it himself, but looked at Leif vaguely.

'Is this—' he began rather hoarsely, cleared his throat and tried again. 'Is this Valhalla?'

'Valhalla?' Leif said. 'What's that?'

'Where the brave Vikings go when they die.'

There was a rustling sound in the hall.

'What's he say? What's he talking about?' the nosey, fascinated watchers asked each other.

'We're not dead,' Leif said. 'This is Runnydale Hall. We live here.'

'Runnydale Hall? What land is this?'

Leif said, 'Please tell me your name.'

'My name? I am Mordec son of Hauk.'

Some other boys had mounted the platform and came up to Mordec son of Hauk, the amazing apparition, to touch his shoulders, feel his hair, poke his chest, testing that he was real and not a phantom. Mordec shrugged them off, pushed them away. 'Stop that,' he protested.

Zarath clapped his hands and five Runners came to do his bidding. 'Help the Orphan and his friend away,' Zarath ordered them, 'to your house. Guard them well.' Runners lifted Leif down from the chair, and shepherded him and Mordec down the steps, through the length of the hall, the crowd applauding again as Mordec passed among them. The doors were opened and Mordec and Leif were taken out into the moonlit night. The doors were closed again firmly to keep the men, women and over-excited children from following.

Zarath thumped the floor of the platform with the wand and called for silence. The chatter of the crowd subsided. When everyone was quiet, they stood looking up at the magician expectantly, their eyes full of questions which they couldn't find the words to ask but hoped he would answer anyway. But Zarath called out masterfully, 'Thank you, my frrriends. Until next year, good-night, good-bye, and may all your *possible* wishes come true.' He bowed a slow, deep, dramatic bow with his arms outspread, and a moment later was gone. The platform was in darkness. The great entertainment was over.

The crowd left peacefully, many saying they would never forget what they had seen tonight. 'How?' and 'Who?' were asked a thousand times and went un-answered as often.

The Lords of Runnydale were as puzzled as the peas-antry. Each of them directed his 'How?' and his 'Who?' at the Princess, not expecting her to understand them, let alone answer them. They had communicated with her through Zarath ever since she had arrived on a ship with a retinue of servants the night before (and had presented each of the lords with a gift of a ceremonial gold chain, and promised to pay for her lodging in the palace with regular gifts of gold). She had apologised for not having an interpreter with her.

'I had one,' she said, 'but lost him on the way.'

To assure her of their goodwill, and reassure her that their words were friendly, both the Rulers smiled continuously at her whenever they looked at her. And she smiled back.

'Astonishing!' said Alger.

'Astounding!' said Humfrey.

'Can Zarath actually magick a Viking across the North Sea?' Alger said to her through his smile.

'And keep him invisible until the moment he must appear at the Granting!' Humfrey exclaimed through his bared teeth.

'Actually, boys,' the Princess suddenly said in perfectly good, if oddly accented, English, 'that Viking boy—there was something about him. I think I've seen him before. Or someone who looked very like him. But that was in Italy.'

'Italy?' Alger said, quickly recovering from his surprise that she could speak English.

'Zarath magicked him here from *Italy*?' Humfrey said, still too amazed by the conjuring of the Viking boy to wonder at his suddenly understanding the Princess, 'He's even better than I'd thought, that Zarath!'

'Well, I don't know for sure if it's the same boy. The one I'm thinking of wore glasses.'

But Alger and Humfrey liked the idea of the boy being magicked all the way from Italy.

'Italy!' they both exclaimed again—looking at each other with wide eyes.

They were so beside themselves with wonder that they forgot for a few seconds that they never talked directly to each other.

They both remembered at the same moment, turned away abruptly, and addressed themselves exclusively to the Princess for the rest of the evening.

in the runners' barn

Runners hardly ever ran. They usually walked at an easy pace, which was lucky for Mordec who felt a little unsteady on his legs as they strolled past stables and sheds and sties and sheepfolds. He couldn't see well though the moon was bright, because he'd lost his glasses somewhere, along with his memory, his bearings, his companions and possibly his life as it had been up until now. He was aware of the coolness of the night, that Leif the Orphan was hanging on to the tattered sleeve of his torn and shabby dark blue tunic, and that the tall thin Runner beside him was asking him questions. But he could spare little thought for what was being said. He was trying hard to recall the last thing that had happened to him before he woke on the mound of sand with lights dazzling him and the scent of flowers in his nostrils.

They entered a barn, a big space lit only by the lazily waving flames of a hearth-fire at one end and the pale still moonlight which fell through the open door. Tables and benches were scattered about. The Runners took off their boots and scarlet cloaks and disposed themselves on benches, still discussing the magic of Zarath. Some thought there must be a trick in it somewhere, others insisted that it was real magic and by definition beyond all explaining.

Mordec sat down beside the lanky Runner on a bench near the fire, shaking his sleeve free from the small hand that gripped it.

'Tell me please,' he said, 'what is this country?'

'Wales, of course,' the Runner—whose name was Flint—replied. 'It's never been anything else. Except in our own language it's always been Cymru.'

'Wales I've heard of. Not Cum-ree,' Mordec said. 'However did I get here?'

'You were magicked,' the Runner said. 'You can't have forgotten. It happened only a few minutes ago.'

Mordec wanted a better explanation than that, but he didn't expect to get it from the Runner.

'So we are near England,' he said.

'Both near and far,' the Runner replied. 'Near in miles, far in spirit.'

'Near in miles? Then I shan't be staying long.'

'Why? Where will you go?'

'To England. At sunrise tomorrow. From there I'll be able to get home.'

'Easier said than done, eh, fellows?' The Runner raised his voice to appeal to his colleagues. 'Boy here says he's going to England tomorrow. Easier said than done, eh?'

A general murmur of assent arose. Some shook their heads.

'There's mountains, you see,' the Runner said.

'Mountains,' other Runners echoed.

'Hard climbing.'

'Hard.'

'You'll take me with you Mordec, won't you?' Leif said.

'I wish I knew how I got here,' Mordec said.

A stout bald Runner with steel pale eyes, wearing a longer and much smarter red cloak than the others wore, came and sat on a bench facing Mordec. He looked at him thoughtfully before saying: 'So you're Mordec son of Hauk, eh? I'm Chief Runner. My name's Slate. Tell me, Mordec son of Hauk, what's the last thing you remember before you woke up in the hall?'

Mordec pondered for some moments then said slowly, 'I was all wet. I was lying on wet sand. Someone else was there, standing near me. Yes, I remember he gave me something to drink. I was thirsty. I asked for water and he gave me something to drink. It tasted funny. Then he or someone else picked me up and carried me somewhere. But I fell asleep before I got wherever he was taking me. To the hall, perhaps. Where I was when I woke.'

'See? It's coming back to you, lad. Give yourself a few days and you'll remember everything.'

'A few days?'

'Or weeks.'

'*Weeks?*'

'Maybe months.'

'*Months!*'

'Years, if you like.'

'YEARS! Here? No no. I must remember at once. Now.'

'Had anything to eat?'

'I don't think so.'

'Hungry?'

'Yes, I am, yes.'

'There's bread and boiled leeks and dried fish-heads on the table, see? Help yourself, lad.'

The Runners were not allowed to eat the fine food that the folk had been given to feast on. The bread was hard, the leeks were tasteless, the fish-heads were scaly and prickly, but Mordec was hungry enough not to care. He washed a few mouthfuls down with jugs of water. Then he flung himself on a stack of straw heaped against the wall and fell into a deep sleep with little Leif sitting beside him and watching over him until he too fell asleep with one arm over Mordec as though to keep him there.

As midnight approached, Slate the Chief Runner stood for a while in the open doorway of the barn watching the last of the long procession of the folk of Runnydale, who on foot or cart or occasional donkey had been streaming home by moonlight for the past two hours. Babies slept in their parent's arms, children slept in the carts. But the grown folk were not weary. They had a sprightliness in their step because, Slate, understood, they were happy. All of them had feasted, some had witnessed a magic show they would never forget, and some had had a wish granted.

Slate yawned and stretched. 'It's what the old Romans used to say,' he told the sinking moon. 'Bread and circuses. To keep the people happy, give them bread and circuses.'

Behind him men slept on benches or straw. Some snored. One muttered. His own body was weary, and he set off for the comfortable bed in his house, his thoughts running on the Viking boy as he went.

So they found him on the seashore. Someone did. Went and told that dear old trickster Zarath, who must have drugged him. The hardest part must have been to judge just how much of a soporific to give the lad so he'd sleep up to the moment he was 'materialized' and not a moment longer. Also hard to judge how much to bribe the helpers not to give the game away. And where had he kept him hidden until the moment of his awakening in the hall? Slate guessed, most likely in the cottage of Dave the Fisher.

In the palace, Humfrey, Alger, and the Princess had all gone to their luxurious quarters and lain themselves down on furs and linen bags full of duck's down, and drifted into sleep—Alger dreamlessly, the Princess still feeling a little peckish, and Humfrey watching a dream ship sail away into the mystic West with Alger on board, never to return.

Zarath sat up late with his feet in a mustard bath, brooding on how lucky he was to have found Mordec. Luck that far, yes, but fast thinking had done the rest. Alerted by Dave the Fisher, whose daughter had gone gathering cockles as soon as the rain stopped, about what she had found among the rocks, he'd seen the possibilities immediately and had acted from then on with smooth mastery. He did not know then that the boy was a Viking. True, Leif's wish, confided to Zarath often, was for another Viking, but he could be talked into wishing aloud at the Granting for anything the boy might have turned out to be. It was the hugest piece of luck, almost enough to persuade Zarath himself that he had magical powers, that the boy was indeed the Viking of Leif's longing.

For the measuring of the potion, though he was out of practice, experience was his teacher and memory his guide.

The mustard bath was growing cold. Zarath sighed, dried his feet, wrapped himself in a bearskin and sank on to a gilded couch that an old friend, Mel de Gustybuss, had once designed and caused to be made for himself, or for a theatrical performance, and had presented to the magician when they'd sadly parted. Mel de Gustybuss was permanently employed by Reginald, Earl of Linkard as his Art Director. He and Zarath had made a brilliant team of drama producers: one with a flair for scenery, the other for illusions.

Zarath would have been happy to stay longer at the Earl's court, but he had a contract with the Lords of Runnydale for three years of 'professional service'. (A contract that had been extended again and again.) It had been negotiated by means of pigeon communication through the agency of a rich Troll named Julius who lived in the Far North and contrived to know everything that was going on everywhere in the Known World and Beyond. He knew the Lords of Runnydale wanted a magician. He knew that Zarath was tired of touring and wanted a stable billet. So an agreement was made, a contract signed. Julius had procured passage for Zarath on a Viking ship, and a short-term contract with the Earl of Linkard for a break in the journey. Eventually on to Runnydale Zarath had had to go.

Six mounted Runners had been sent by ship and road with a low cart by the Lords of Runnydale to fetch him from Earl Reginald's court where he had spent so happy a season. He and his baggage were drawn on the cart to the port of London, and from there an English ship had borne him and his escort round the south of England and up the west coast of Wales to Runnydale. Fishing boats had ferried him to the small harbour where, on the jetty, Alger and Humfrey stood well apart from each other waiting to greet him. Zarath had managed to this day to remain on excellent terms with both of them, always listening sympathetically to their complaints about each other without ever uttering one himself.

With him and his chests of professional equipment had come also the gilded couch on which, this beautiful moonlit night, Zarath at last slept peacefully, his heart and mind solaced with success.

adrift

The instant Mordec woke, he remembered.

Low-curling smoke entered the ship's dark hatch in which he lay. He breathed it in and coughed. He was hot, his eyes smarted, his glasses were gone, his head was sore and he could feel a swollen lump on it. All he wanted was to get out to the air. Still coughing, he crawled about feeling for the doors, and he found them, tightly closed. Some heavy solid thing was pressing against them on the outside. Only smoke could get through them, and the smoke must mean that the ship was on fire! 'Help,' he tried to shout, but made only a croaking sound which turned into another racking cough. He could hear the noise of something knocking out there on the deck, but it was irregular and did not suggest the presence of anybody who could hear him even if he had been able to shout.

The ship was burning and he was trapped. For a few moments he was gripped by terror, unable to move. But then, as at other times in his life when he had felt afraid—he ordered himself to 'keep calm and think'.

'Think—if something was moved against the doors it can be moved away again. All you can do is push.'

He was still dazed, but urged on by the terror of being choked and burnt in that low dark prison, he managed to push hard enough to force whatever was blocking the doors to give way a little. He must go on pushing, but had to pause every time a cough shook his whole body though he knew he mustn't waste a moment.

He put his back to the doors, counted to five, took a deep breath while holding the sleeve of his tunic against his nose to filter the smoke, and pushed again with all his might. Again the thing pressing on the other side of them shifted. A thin line of dim light showed through the opening between the two leaves of the door.

He turned and used his arms until they were shaking with the effort, putting all the strength of his body be-hind them, all the power of his desperation, and he felt the thing sliding, the doors yielding, and suddenly one of them opened all the way. He was out in a moment, free, clambering to his feet, coughing as if he would bring his lungs up. Alive. And he meant to stay that way.

With stinging watering eyes he looked about him, but could see little more than smoke swirling low over the deck and the top of the mainmast in a blurred pale light, perhaps of early morning.

Slowly as the swirls cleared away in patches, he made out the bare, scorched boards, heaps of things reduced to still smoking ashes, and a line of busy flame where a last remaining sail was still alight.

'Hullo!' he tried to shout, his voice coming out hoarse and quavering. He cleared his scorched throat as best he could, cupped his hands round his mouth and tried again: 'Hullo? Anybody there?'

No answer. He was alone on a burning ship. No crew, no sails. Yet the ship was moving. Swiftly and smoothly she was sailing away from the brighter east. So towards England, he hoped. But if there was land not far out there to the West, he knew he wouldn't be able to see it with his unaided eyes even in broad day-light, until it loomed so close that the ship would be in danger of running aground, perhaps to wreck on reefs of rock—and that, he thought ruefully, would be the end of him. But for the moment he was in-expressibly glad just to be alive and breathing air.

He clearly enough saw the object which had blocked the doors: a water-barrel, which changed a moment later from enemy to friend, for when he peered into he found it was full of rainwater. Using his hands to scoop it up, he drank, not minding that it tasted of ash.

He inspected every part of the ship. He found no one else alive on her and—what was more surprising considering that it had been Bjarwulf leading the raid—no one dead.

The handle of the rudder was so burnt that it crumbled at a touch. The sails were destroyed, the mainmast scorched. But the oak timbers of the ship were intact.

He wondered why the pirates had decided to try and scuttle her rather than keep her. They had stripped her almost bare. The only moveable things that re-mained as far as he could see were the water-barrel and some tin lanterns that rolled this way and that with the rise and fall of the ship on the restless sea. Everything else, including his own bundles of books and spare eyeglasses, was gone. The two small rowing-boats were gone. The cargoes were gone, and the stores of food—except for some heads of garlic.

He broke off a clove, peeled it, and nibbled it, sitting on the seat by the useless rudder. And that was when he first began to ask the question: who had knocked him on the head, pushed him into the hatch, taken his things, and then shut him in? Someone strong enough to push a full water-barrel over the deck and hard up against the doors. It must have been done while the pirate raid was on.

Had someone tried to save him from the pirates? Who might do that? Lily? She was strong but not strong enough to move the barrel. And why would she hit him on the head? No. Whoever had done it had wanted him to die. If not from the blow then from—what? The fire? Someone had shut him in the hatch when the ship had been set on fire? Not just wanting him to die, but to die a terrible death! Who could that person be? One of the pirates? They did not seem to have killed anyone else, so why him? Who had reason to want to kill him? Who had quarreled with him? Could it have been Olaf who wanted to claim ownership of Foal of the Foam, the small ship Mordec had found? No. Olaf had seemed pleased to see him, and none of the other pirates had any cause to hate him. So who had it been? And why hadn't Gus or Lily looked for him before sailing away, made sure he was with them?

He was safe on the ship if he could reach land before he died of hunger. Safe as long as water was in the barrel and if rain came to refill it when it was empty.

He searched the ship again, looking in places he had not known were there under loose timbers, and found, to his huge delight, a fishing rod—one of his own that he had brought on the voyage with him. Now with a bit of luck he would get himself food. Raw, but sustaining.

Rain did fall. The warm ashy liquid in the barrel changed to cool fresh water. He stripped and let the rain wash his body, and spread his tunic on the deck to let the rain launder it.

He did catch a few fish, but one of them poisoned him. He felt ill for hours, and wondered if now he would die. Many times he leant over the side to be sick on the sea, and each time the mess brought a school of minnows to devour it. He wondered if they would be poisoned too, or whether their tiny guts could digest it.

At night he slept beside the mainmast, cradling his face in his arms. Days passed and nights passed—he couldn't remember how many.

One damp, overcast morning he woke to find that the Good Ship Good was squatting on a sand shelf within wading distance of a rocky beach. The sharp peaks of rocks rose out of the shallows like giant spearheads in all directions, so it had been by sheer luck that the tide had borne her between them, and her flat bottom had kept her from being scraped open by more of them invisible in the water. When the tide ebbed, it left The Good Ship Good on a sand bar.

Mordec did not even get his shins wet when he walked ashore.

But within a few minutes he was soaked head to toe by a sudden heavy rainfall that dropped out of the sky as though a giant had emptied a vast pitcher over the beach.

He sought shelter under a rocky overhang. The sand he sat on was hard and uncomfortable. After a while the rain fell less heavily, but persisted for hours. The tide came in, and he saw the Good Ship Good being carried out to sea again.

'I'm hungry. There must be people living some-where around here,' he mused. 'I could offer to do some work for them for the wage of a meal.'

But the rain became heavy again.

He crossed his arms tightly, dropped his head on his chest, and though he was cold, and the rain dripped onto his feet, he soon fell into a doze.

hauk's oath

Olaf son of Olaf the Shipbuilder led Bjarwulf the Pirate—huddled in a cloak of bearskin that concealed whatever weapons usually hung about his body, his hank of hair on the crown of his otherwise shaved head tied in a knot and for the nonce not decorated with its golden arrow, his ears and nose free of their gold and silver rings, even his formerly long moustaches clipped modestly short, so that he looked almost like other men—to the door of Hauk the Meadmaker. When Hauk opened it to their knock, the boy entered behind the pirate and stood looking down. As was the custom when an important message was to be delivered, the visitors remained standing, and their very refusal to sit was in itself a warning to Hauk and his wife Estrid that they brought bad news.

Hauk tried to shut out the first thought that came to him—'They're about to tell me that Mordec is dead'—but he commanded himself to stand silent and listen. Estrid sat still as a statue, the same thought, born of love and terror, tearing through her head and freezing her heart. Even little Eyrin, their infant son, knew that this was a moment for keeping still and saying nothing. He leant against his mother and stared wide-eyed at the big hairy man with the bushy black eyebrows and beard as he told his brief tale.

Bjarwulf, hanging his head, said gruffly but as meekly as a rough boastful pirate could, 'Your son Mordec is lost at sea. I am sorry to bring you this news.'

There was silence for a long moment. Hauk and Estrid looked at each other. Bjarwulf and Olaf continued to look at the floor. Then Hauk said, 'Tell us what happened.'

Bjarwulf's story was brief. He could only tell what he knew and that was little; simply that Mordec had been found on a ship he and his prentice boys had raided, that young Olaf had recognized Mordec at once with surprise and pleasure, and when the cargo and crew and—he'd thought—all the passengers, including Mordec, Gus son of Hakon, and the young Queen of the Fenreach, had been taken on to the Serpent King or Foal of the Foam, they'd sailed on, having set fire to The Good Ship Good and abandoning her to the wind and waves, to scuttle or sail as the gods decided, being an empty shell, or so they'd all believed. Those on the Serpent King—Bjarwulf and his pirates, and the woman Captain of the abandoned ship, and the woman Captain's woman Mate, and the English Queen, and most of the all-girl crew of The Good Ship Good—had simply assumed that Mordec and Gus were both with the boys on Foal of the Foam.

'And at the same time the boys,' Bjarwulf said, stretching out a thick hairy jewelled hand towards

Olaf as representative of the full complement of boys, 'thought he must be aboard the Serpent King with the English Queen, as they were good friends. Not so, Olaf?'

Olaf nodded dumbly without looking up.

It was only—Bjarwulf went on—when they reached England to put some of the women ashore that they discovered Mordec was not with them.

Hauk and Estrid heard him out, waited for more, and when no more came, Hauk spoke.

'Mordec,' he began hoarsely. He paused to clear his throat and began again, sounding very calm: 'Mordec is unlikely to fall overboard. So you are telling me that he was left on a burning ship. Is that what you're saying?'

'I'm sorry to bring you such news,' Bjarwulf said.

'You are sure that's what happened?'

'Yes.'

'Did you try to find the ship when you realized what had happened?'

Bjarwulf shrugged helplessly. His gesture eloquently implied: 'How could we hope to find the ship? Where should we start looking? How long should we have tried? I couldn't find anything, I haven't found anything, here we are without Mordec, and with our grave news that we have lost him.'

'Tell me how it happened,' Hauk demanded. 'If Mordec saw you casting off without him he would have hailed you, shouted for you to wait for him.'

Bjarwulf knew the reason why Mordec had not seen them draw away, and had not shouted out, for on the voyage home from England, Gus had told him what he'd done. But before he answered he swallowed hard, cleared his throat, shifted his weight from one foot to the other and finally said, with a frown, as seriously and ponderously as a judge summing up a piece of disturbing evidence that been put before him as an objective observer: 'It seems he was locked up.'

On hearing this, Estrid gripped Eyrin's hand so tightly that the boy looked up at her in sudden fear.

'How—she began, but Hauk cut her short by exclaiming with force: 'Locked up! How could he have been locked up? Why? Who did it? Was he a prisoner on the raided ship? Olaf—you saw him—was he locked up then? Why didn't you release him? Are you telling me you took the ship but didn't rescue my son from enemy capture?'

As Hauk's wrath grew, Olaf opened and shut his mouth and looked at Bjarwulf, and Bjarwulf raised both his jewelled hands to beg for his patience.

'No, no, Hauk, that's not how it was. He was a passenger. His grandfather had paid for him and Gus and the English Queen to sail to England. He was free. *We didn't know* he was locked up. At least most of us didn't know. I didn't and—

'I didn't,' Olaf said, raising his eyebrows and wrinkling up his forehead to show how innocent he was as he briefly looked up at Hauk and then Estrid before dropping his gaze to the floor again, his face burning red.

'Who did know? Someone must have known—whoever did it knew. Did the crew lock him up because your raid made him into an enemy and a possible hostage?' Hauk was frowning with the effort to think how it could have happened. 'No—he would have put up a fight. Did he put up a fight? Was there a battle?'

'There was a battle, but that wasn't how—wasn't why … Olaf, tell them. Tell them who did it.'

Olaf raised his still burning face and looked at Estrid as he blurted out, 'Gus son of Hakon did it. But he only told us after we'd reached England. The rest of us didn't know, honestly we didn't. Not till he told us. We thought—

Hauk interrupted, frowning again most thunderously. 'Gus son of Hakon? Are you saying that Mordec's friend deliberately locked Mordec up so that he couldn't escape from a burning ship?'

Again Olaf hung his head. In truth he felt almost as ashamed as if he'd done it himself, though he couldn't have said why.

'That is what happened,' Bjarwulf said. Then he added in as sympathetic a tone as a man could manage who had never really had much sympathy with anyone, 'I'm sorry. Very sorry.' And he cleared his throat again.

Hauk said, 'Gus himself told you that he'd done this?'

The faces and the silence of Bjarwulf and Olaf were answer enough.

Hauk turned his back on them to hide his feelings, and saw on his wife's face the dismay he felt himself. He swung round again to face the pirate and in a low tone in which controlled grief and restrained fury were mixed in equal measure, said: 'But why? What injury had my son done Gus son of Hakon that such merciless revenge was taken?'

Bjarwulf took a step towards Hauk and laid a hand on his shoulder. 'We hold the son of Hakon bound. He himself must answer your questions and later he'll answer to the Thing for his crime.'

At that moment the fate of Gus was not uppermost in the minds of Hauk and Estrid. But to find out all they could about the events which had brought Mordec to his dire peril was their immediate need, so Hauk cried out, 'Where is he? Where is this Gus, this son of Hakon, this would-be murderer of my son?'

'Held in the shipyard. His father is with him, waiting for you,' Olaf said hurriedly as he felt Hauk's anger mounting.

'Go tell them we are coming.'

Bjarwulf went to the door but hesitated with his hand on the latch. 'Hauk,' he said, looking round, 'if I'm partly to blame for what happened—'

'Until I know the whole story I can't say where blame lies,' Hauk said, and Bjarwulf and Olaf left without another word.

When they'd gone, Estrid and Hauk stood for a while with their arms about each other saying nothing. Eyrin buried his face in his mother's clothes.

'Come,' Hauk said at last. 'Let's go and hear all about it. And then ...'

His voice sounded so determined, Estrid looked up at him and searched his face for a sign of hope, and repeated, 'And then?'

'I'll go and find him,' Hauk finished, 'I'll search sea and land until I find him and bring him home. On my oath, by Thor, I'll not come home without him.'

He did not say, 'I'll bring him home dead or alive.'

It was plain that Hauk would not even consider the possibility that Mordec was dead. And neither would Mordec's mother.

the confession

Gus had had time enough on the voyage home to think about what he'd done. He saw it now as an act of madness. He couldn't stop reproaching himself. Eating little, sleeping little, he accused himself, with disgust, of the same crimes and stupidities over and over again, asking himself questions without answers. How could jealousy have driven him to such an extreme act of cruelty against his friend? After all, he really liked Mordec, thought him by far the best of all the boys he knew. Did Lily really care for Mordec more than she did for him? He wasn't sure that she did. And even if she did, would such a deed on his part make her change her mind? And even if she did like Mordec more, there was still the question whether Mordec cared for her to the same degree. And even if the two of them had an understanding between them, and even if they had been plotting together against him, and even if he had known this for sure, what he had done would not have been right. A Viking didn't send another Viking to shipwreck and death even if he had good reason to believe himself wronged. It was not only unjust, it was also cowardly, and a coward was the lowest thing a Viking could be.

So Gus's shame was great. He said so to his father; and Hakon the Tanner felt tainted by his son's crime and dishonour, and shared his shame.

When Hauk, followed by Estrid holding Eyrin's hand, came into the shed where Gus sat rope-bound in the sawdust, a crowd of men and boys were already assembled there, Bjarwulf and Olaf among them. They made way for the family of the lost boy, some offering a few words of sympathy, some patting Hauk's back in a gesture of fellowship as he passed by.

Hauk stopped before Gus, and Gus looked up, half expecting a blow and determined not to shrink from it. No one, least of all Hakon, the huge yellow-headed, yellow-bearded man who stood beside his son, would have tried to stop Hauk from striking him, only from killing him. Hakon drank a lot (he was one of Hauk's best customers), but he was sober now. He knew that only by submitting to judgment could he save a shred of his family's honour, though they lose all else to pay Hauk the compensation he was entitled to for Mordec's murder: the Wergeld.

But Hauk kept his hands at his sides. Beside him stood Estrid and Eyrin. All three watched Gus's thin, drawn face, which showed remorse but not fear. Estrid was sure that the boy deeply and painfully regretted what he'd done, and at this moment the sight of him roused her, not to pity, but more to wonder than to rage.

Hauk was brief and calm, if also grim.

'Tell me,' he said.

'I tried to kill Mordec,' Gus said. 'He was in the hold when the ship was set on fire. I stunned him first.'

A murmur of surprise, anger, disgust went through the crowd.

'I blocked the door of the hold so even if he awoke before the fire reached him or the ship sank he would not be able to escape.'

Hakon closed his eyes, threw back his head and whimpered sharply like a wounded wolf.

'I took his glasses from him, and wore them as I sat among the others in Foal of the Foam. I knew that Lily—that someone might look for him and I thought that as they wouldn't be able to see very well in the flickering light of the burning ship, if they caught a glimpse of someone wearing glasses they would think it must be Mordec.'

'Go on,' Hauk said, still calm, still grim. He did not ask why. An answer to why, and whether it was an answer of any worth, was for the Thing to find out. For Hauk there could be no explanation that would lessen in the least degree the enormity that had been done to Mordec.

'That's all. That's what I did. We sailed away. When we landed on the English coast they found that Mordec was not with us and I told them then what I had done. They bound me and brought me back to tell you and to be tried at the Thing. I …' He swallowed hard. 'I am very sorry for what I did … I … I hope Mordec found a way out. I … I …'

He hung his head in shame and said no more.

Hauk said nothing in reply. He turned away abruptly to ask Bjarwulf a question.

'I need to know,' he said, speaking like a captain, a chief, a man whose authority could not be questioned, 'where you were when you parted from the raided ship. Which way it would have drifted. All you can tell me of the winds and tides.'

Then he turned to Olaf the Shipbuilder. 'I need a ship.' He looked round at the faces of the men. 'And a crew. Tonight we'll meet in the mead hall, as many as will, to talk more about this.'

He had started for the door when Hakon stepped forward and called out for all to hear: 'Hauk, my son's shame is my shame. It's for you to say what must be done with him now—what his punishment will be after the judgment of the Thing.'

Hauk looked down again at Gus, considering. He would have liked to ask the boy—whose truthfulness he strangely still trusted—to tell him all that had happened to him and Mordec since they had set out to help Lily find her mother. But at once a better thought came to him: 'I'll wait to hear Mordec tell the tale.'

So he said to the men, 'Keep him safe until we return with Mordec. I'm not the one to say what his punishment must be. Mordec is. He is fifteen and it's his right and his duty.'

to the rescue

That night all the men gathered in the mead hall, sombre in mood. Though they drank deep as always, they did not become wild, they sang no songs and never once laughed. Loss and shame bit them all.

Hauk asked to be heard and they listened in silence.

'You all know,' Hauk said, 'that my son has been lost at sea. I want men to sail with me to find him. It won't be easy, and it will take time. I am asking much of you, but nothing that I would not do for any one of you who found himself in this sad state in which I find myself forlornly flung. You are all good seamen. You are all brave. And you are all honourable. Yes, all of you!' And he looked directly at Hakon as he said this.

Hakon lifted his head and met Hauk's eyes, and Hauk knew then that one at least had made up his mind to accompany him on his difficult quest.

'If any man chooses not to come, I shall not hold it against him, nor think any the worse of him. The season is late, the voyage may be perilous, we have no certain destination, and no day set for return. I can only promise this: those who come with me will not go unrewarded. I am not a poor man, and although I cannot pay out treasure like a king, and the voyage itself is unlikely to lead us to new riches, no one who lends his strength and risks his life and limb to aid me now will be the poorer for it if he lives, and if he does not, I will not forget his wife and children. Tonight no one pays for the ale they drink or the mead. Nor tomorrow night when I ask those of you who will sail with me to meet here again and help me plan the voyage. Whether few come with me or many, sail and search I shall until I have found my son Mordec.'

They cheered him then, one quick cheer, and left.

The next night Hauk went early to the mead hall and waited patiently though anxiously to see who would come. It seemed to him a long wait. He began to fear that no one—not even Hakon for all his shame—was willing to risk a long voyage at this time of year to search the vast ocean for a lost boy.

What with brooding and drinking and keeping himself tense with hope, he became weary at last and almost fell into a doze. So he was startled when the door was flung open with such force that it banged against the wall, and in strode Hakon followed by a stream of men. He had gathered all the grown and able-bodied men of the fjord—craftsmen, farmers, traders, who were also every one of them warriors and sailors—to come to offer help of all sorts.

Hauk looked up, relief spreading over his face and running through him like a first drink of mead at the end of a dry day.

He rose smiling, and when all of them stood before him he spread his arms and laughed with relief and gratitude. They laughed with him. Then they drank heartily, Hauk refilling the jugs as often as they emptied them. They sang, they danced like bears until some fell down and slept, snoring, until morning.

In the sober light of the next day, twenty-one men came to the shipyard to offer their services to Hauk. They would be enough. One ship would be enough, but every man on board must be a fine sailor.

All of them were that. And these willing friends, twenty of them were the men he knew best, the companions of his youth who had sailed with him in his raiding days. The one exception was Hakon the Tanner, father of Gus. And he, though by nature wild and rough, had most reason to prove himself dependable in Hauk's service, to atone for his son's misdeed. He needed to do this, and Hauk must let him.

So Hauk walked straight up to him, the two men looked each other in the eyes, and when Hakon nodded, Hauk clapped his shoulder and moved on. The others he embraced, one by one.

When Olaf the shipbuilder offered to let him have a ship for a low charge, Hauk accepted the offer, thanked him, and then added: 'Will you also let me have your son? I am not asking any other boys to come, but your son is already dedicated to a life at sea.'

'He is fifteen,' Olaf replied. 'It is for him to choose. If he agrees, I will not stand in his way.'

The next morning Hauk began his preparations for a long absence. Estrid took over the care of the orchard and beehives, and the mead-making, and the overseeing of the five thralls.

He came and went at odd hours of the short dim days and the lengthening nights without telling Estrid what progress was being made.

'Aren't you wasting time, dear?' she asked him. 'Shouldn't you start—

'I have started,' he told her. 'Everything I'm doing is to help me find him.'

Hauk had to gather supplies for a long voyage in a season when few ventured on voyages. He spent hours in the shipyard deciding with Olaf what vessel to choose. The one they thought best was built for trade rather than for speed and battle, because he would need ample space for the supplies of a long voyage.

He was in the yard looking it over with the ship-builder when Bjarwulf hailed them and shouted, while still some way off, 'My ship, Meadmaker.'

Hauk and the shipbuilder looked at each other.

'His would be best,' Big Olaf said. 'It's the only ship I ever built that can carry big cargoes and yet float in shallow seas. It can also turn fast for its size, and if it's still as it was when I last looked it over, it's tighter than any ship in the yard.'

Bjarwulf came up to them smiling, cocksure of what he meant to do.

'You'll sail with us. Me and my men. We've decided. There's room for you and more because most of them are needed at home in the winter. But some say their wives won't miss them more than usual.'

Bjarwulf himself was reputed to have three 'wives', but everyone knew that if he did, it was certain none of them lived with him and his slaves and his crew in his sprawling house, some miles north of Trygghaven, where he had his own harbour and vast warehouse on a half-hidden inlet that he himself had named Lovehaven—whether for the love of wives or humankind in general, no one knew.

Hauk needed to think awhile about Bjarwulf's offer, understand clearly what was being proposed.

'But—if I sail with you, it can't be on the mere chance that we find Mordec. I mean I can't wait while you stop to make raids. Or take the sort of risks you take.'

'No raids,' Bjarwulf said, shaking his head vigorously. 'We sail only to search. Nothing will stop us. You'll be safe with me. No one attacks my ship. And I'll attack nothing—until after we've got him, anyway. Maybe on the way home—no? As you wish. I'll bring you and him home first before I do anything else. So what do you say?'

Hauk thanked him but asked him to wait a few hours for an answer. The shipbuilder urged him to accept.

Estrid was not sure at first. 'Pirates are reckless by nature,' she said.

'It'll be safe enough if nothing comes along to tempt him,' Hauk said. 'And he'd charge me even less than the shipbuilder—just the cost of the extra supplies. He's had rich plunder lately. They say he wears more gold and silver to sleep in than a king at his crowning.'

Estrid suggested that they list the Fors and Againsts. So Hauk started with the Fors, marking them off on his fingers: the ship was sound, it was ready to sail, the men were used to being at sea for weeks or even months on end, they were fine seamen, brave, enduring, experienced—.

'Four,' Eyrin said. Estrid had recently taught him to count, and he liked doing it.

'Now the Againsts,' said Estrid after a pause.

Hauk again put his right forefinger to the little finger of his left hand. 'Well,' he said, and paused again.

'No Againsts?' Estrid said.

'Ah yes, just one,' said Hauk. 'But it's a big one. I wouldn't be in charge.'

'Make sure then that he'll do what you ask, go where you want, put your needs first. Make sure before you accept his offer,' she advised.

Bjarwulf gave the assurances that Hauk wanted. 'The only thing that'll come before your needs are the needs of the ship. There my word alone must rule.'

'Fair enough. So we're agreed, and I am in your debt,' said Hauk.

'Not so,' Bjarwulf growled. 'Wasn't I in part to blame that Mordec was left behind? Be ready soon. We must start with all the speed the winter winds can give us.'

Hauk smiled, despite his anxiety, and warmly shook the hand of the pirate. Now much of the preparation for the voyage could be left in his capable hands.

Among Bjarwulf's customary preparations for a voyage, was a consultation with his kinsman Sigvald, the blind Skald and seer. His predictions decided the day and the hour of departure, all else such as the wind, tide and weather being equally favorable. The Skald's approval made all the pirates feel safe. A little priestly pleading with Thor was usually also sought, though the priest and the Skald regarded each other with a sceptical eye, each thinking the other to be a bit of a humbug (and both of them, in Estrid's opinion, being right).

Having heard the Skald's sage opinion, Bjarwulf sent him to Hauk.

Sigvald arrived at Hauk's gate in the bullock-cart of Hrut the Trader, and for an hour he wandered with the Meadmaker, followed by Estrid and Hrut, among the trees of the orchard with one hand clutching a beaker of ale and the other touching the trees for news from the world of unseen spirits, and found himself able to paint a picture in words of the land where Mordec had come ashore.

'Aaah!' sighed the Skald. 'I'm sorry to say … Are you sure you want to know?'

'I suppose so,' Estrid said.

'Yes, please,' Eyrin said.

'Well, if you'd rather not …' Hauk began.

'Then I shall tell you,' the Skald said hastily, 'as you insist. It is a barren, uninhabited land, full of wild ravenous man-eating beasts, offering little shelter and no easy provender. It is a land to test a man's endurance. But …' He raised his voice and a finger. 'I could sell you a charm that would help protect you from the beasts if ever you come to those perilous shores.'

'How much?' Hauk asked—which surprised Estrid for a moment, but then she saw that this would be the quickest way of ending the fruitless interview.

'One quarter cask of mead, two large jugs of honey.'

'Done,' said Hauk and shook the Skald's hand.

Hauk fetched the goods and stowed them on Hrut's cart.

Sigvald solemnly handed him a large sack of charcoal.

'What's this?' Hauk said, 'Charcoal? What do we do with it? Eat it?'

'Darken you hands and faces with it,' Sigvald said in a low conspiratorial tone. 'Frighten the beasts. Don't worry. It will work. It's not your ordinary charcoal. I've chanted special spells over it.'

Hauk and Estrid listened politely but didn't dare to meet each other's eyes in case they burst out laughing. Which was what Eyrin did at the thought of all the blackened faces, much to the annoyance of the Skald who said that he was a bold child and would come to the same sort of calamitous end as his big brother if his parents didn't teach him proper respect for great men and their sacred visions and powers of enchantment.

When he spoke of Mordec's 'calamitious end' and seemed to be assuming that he had already met it, Hauk and Estrid became quite certain that the Skald was the old fake they had always thought him. But they thanked their visitor for the wonderfully clear guidance he had given Hauk of just what sort of a place he must expect—and dread—to find.

Before he drove the Skald away, Hrut the Trader pressed something wrapped in cloth into Hauk's hand which he said was a talisman sent by his daughter Thorgerd to bring them luck on the search and the homecoming.

'When Thorgerd heard that Mordec was lost, she wept,' Hrut said.

'Thank her, and tell her we know that Mordec is safe—and we'll bring him home for sure,' Hauk said.

'What is it?' Eyrin wanted to know as soon as the cart dipped out of sight and they'd stopped waving.

'Let's go in and unwrap it,' Hauk said.

They laid the small parcel on a table and unwound the woollen cloth.

The talisman was a child's chain bracelet, each of its links made of silver, with a broken clasp and one long solid silver link engraved with a name: LEIF. On the back of the long link was the letter M with a minute disc of gold on each of its peaks.

'Must be quite valuable,' Hauk said. 'I wonder where Thorgerd found it. I'll put it in my purse.'

bjarwulf gets his way

Bjarwulf the Pirate, Terror of the Seas, was a man dependent on advice.

And Pelf, his accountant, a small, frail, thin-haired man without whom, Bjarwulf knew very well, he could not succeed in his risky profession, advised him not to undertake this uncharacteristic mission. They were arguing about it in Bjarwulf's well-stocked warehouse.

'I've promised Hauk, so that's that,' Bjarwulf said in what he hoped was a brook-no-argument tone of voice. But he avoided meeting Pelf's eye.

'You've never defied me like this before, Bjarwulf!' Pelf said, shaking his head sadly, as he put away his parchments and abacus, preparing to leave the warehouse at the end of a working day.

He had been studying some letters they'd found on The Good Ship Good addressed by 'Adam the Lombard at Gaudium Brevis Italia to Saul the Lombard at London England'.

He could not make head or tail of them. They had no words other than the names of people he had no knowledge of, but many numbers. Some of the numbers were in columns, added up—correctly, he found. So these could be accounts of money, such as he kept for Bjarwulf and himself. But why anyone would want to send accounts to another country, he could not think. He had a hunch that these letters were profitable for someone, but he could not fathom how. In themselves they were worth nothing to him and Bjarwulf, yet he could not bring himself to throw them away. Somehow, he resolved, he would find out what they were all about. He felt teased and irritated by his failure.

'Well, there's always a first time,' Bjarwulf retorted pertly. 'Now you know that I have a mind of my own. I'm not putty in your hands.'

'Why, it's an act of charity!' Pelf groaned. Nothing was more dismal to Pelf than charity. To his mind, it was a one-word plot against the only occupation worth pursuing—the noble business of accumulating wealth.

'No, not entirely!' Bjarwulf pleaded. 'I'm bound to come across some merchantman to make the voyage worth while.'

'But you promised the Meadmaker you wouldn't do any pirating.'

'Before we find his son. That's what I promised. No pirating before we find the boy. Honestly, Pelf! After that, when the lad's safe aboard, on the way home …' And Bjarwulf spread his arms expansively to indicate how free he would be then, and bared his sharpened teeth and gums which retained here and there traces of the blood-red berry stain he'd rub on them just before a raid to intensify his victims' respect for him.

But Pelf looked unconvinced, unpersuaded, un-mollified, and disdainful.

'Besides,' Bjarwulf said brusquely, dropping the effort to be charming since it didn't work with Pelf, 'Hauk is paying.'

'Expenses only. Larder supplies. The crew will all be volunteers. So why? Give me a reason why you are doing this when you know it's wrong.'

'You don't have to come if you don't want to,' Bjarwulf said, feeling got at.

'You're right I don't have to, and I won't. No point,' Pelf said as he made for the door.

Bjarwulf silently mouthed 'Hoity-toity!' at Pelf's retreating back. Then, 'Ask her what she thinks,' Bjarwulf called after him. 'She'll tell you I ought to do this.'

Bjarwulf meant Pelf's wife, to whom Pelf now went home; his tall, white-haired, poetically mournful, mariner wife Delfinola, whom first he'd seen when he'd boarded The Good Ship Good to advise Bjarwulf on what to plunder from it.

Delfinola coddled him. And while she pretended he was master over her, she knew and he knew that he would actually give way to her. Theirs was a very happy marriage.

Delfinola knelt to take off his leather shoes—buffed to a shine by her own hands—and replace them with the sheepskin slippers she had warmed before the fire, while Pelf told her about his difference of opinion with his Captain.

'He wants to know what you think. He seems to think that you will tell me to go with him.'

'Does he now?' said Delfinola defiantly, standing tall and putting her fists on her hips 'Well let himself come and say that to my face if he dare.'

When Bjarwulf did knock on the door a little later, the good wife welcomed him kindly, seated him by the fire and brought him a glass of the green wine he himself had acquired dishonestly from The Good Ship Good, and of which Pelf had received his customary share.

'Your good man,' Bjarwulf said, baring is red-streaked teeth to look affable, 'would rather I never took the ship upon the waves unless the voyage be profitable. He doesn't think I should take Hauk on an uncertain quest to find his son who may or may not be alive. He says if I go he'll not come with me. I don't suppose you could persuade him? Thing is, if we do come across a merchantman I'll need him.'

'I persuade him? I would not be so bold as to try,' Delfinola said, seating herself on a stool beside her husband's chair and leaning her shoulder against his knee.

'Right. Tell him, tell him,' Pelf urged her.

'Captain,' she said in a soft respectful tone, 'your wealth is growing and growing, and with each voyage you make it greater.'

'Right. Yes. Tell him,' Pelf repeated.

'I'll tell you why you cannot have too much,' she said, and rose, and walked about the house, her voice becoming full-throated as she began to enjoy the tale she told.

'My grandmother's grandmother, Kathleen, who was taller even than I and more beautiful than the night sky, sold her jewels, her lands, forests full of rare birds, her little towns, her green farms, and her lakes full of gold and silver fish, and gave the money to the poor. And, well may you ask, was she happier then than before? And I must in all truth tell you that the answer is neither yes nor no, but in a manner of speaking it is both. Yes, she was happier not to have to look after so many possessions. But, mark my words, having less to do, she found the hours tedious and the days very long.'

Bjarwulf listened attentively, waiting to have the moral of the story drawn for him, and by its light learn whether he should or should not take Hauk on the sea in search of Mordec.

'The dear lady, Kathleen was her name, never thought to enquire why so many people were poor, or point them the way to making riches of their own. All she did, she unloaded her burdens and gave them money, like rain from heaven. Of course, they had not the least idea what to do with it. Oh, there was a dreadful squandering of wealth my grandmother's grandmother set in motion, a long drunkenness, gaming night and day, and in the end the poor were poor again. I am glad to be able to tell you though, that the good man who bought the property of Kathleen, whose name was Ardan Cool-Eye, used it well, and himself gave her the job of the running of the estates that once had been her own, and she did the job a good deal better for him than she had done it for herself, because she had learnt how dreary it was to have nothing to do.'

'Did they get married?' asked her hard-headed husband in whom she had unintentionally created a streak of sentimental weakness at the very moment he'd set eyes on her in the midst of a raid at sea.

'Oh no,' Delfinola said, 'They never knew the joy of it, of a coming together, of a love that would endure the test of time. They were far too busy for any such shenanigans. There's a lot of work in keeping farms and forests and stocking lakes and getting the poor to pay their taxes.'

'So I … you think I ought …?' Bjarwulf prompted her.

'Captain,' Delfinola said, standing before him and looking down into his black eyes, 'I myself long to be back at sea. Often and often I tell you truly I think of the old days on The Good Ship Good, and there are times, they come upon me, when I miss the company of my captain, Mistress of The Good Ship Good, Anwid, who was my friend.'

'Are you saying you want to come with us on the voyage to find the boy?'

'Nooo. Not if my husband is not coming,' She paced about behind their chairs. 'Oh, no, no, no! We will not be parted! But you now. You have given your word. The word of a Viking. You will go and scour the unfriendly seas, and many a lonely place you'll come upon, and many a disappointment will be lying in wait for you to bring a sad lowering of your spirits. But you will press on, strong against the evil spirits of the deep, and you will find the boy at last, in the black dark of the winter, and bring him safe home to his grieving mother. And if the luck is on your side, as it usually is, you will pick up a cargo so rich and copious, 'twill many times over justify your brave endeavor that will be sung about still in the mead hall a hundred years from now, for such will be your fame.'

'So you are saying I should go?'

'And when the voyage is over, here again we'll be, and my darling will reckon up the value of your hoard as ever he has and ever he will, faithful to the end.'

And so it was settled that when Bjarwulf the Pirate set out on his perilous voyage as the year was coming to its close, Pelf would be on board as usual, though afterwards Pelf could never remember how the decision had been made as he had started out being quite set against it.

And what was more, his sea-faring wife would be with him. He understood this when he watched her packing his sea-chest with warm clothes for both of them.

'You are coming with me?' he asked her.

'As you wish, dear,' she said meekly. Though he could not recall having wishes it.

what a viking can do

The Lord Alger had Mordec brought to him as he wallowed, plump and rosy, in his morning bath. Two attendants, an older man and one young enough to be his son, both with shaved heads and both wearing white aprons, were busy topping up the bath water with copper kettles brought from their hooks over a spritely fire, adding more flowers from a basket on the floor, hanging towels over a wooden horse before the grate, placing a pair of morocco slippers on the woven grass mat beside the tub, and laying out the Lord's clothes.

'Come in, boy. Stand over there where I can see you. Now—what is your name?'

'Mordec son of Hauk.'

'And you are a Viking?'

'I am, illustrious lord.'

'Is that a title you use when addressing Viking chiefs?'

'Only when addressing rulers of the land, Kings and Conquerors.'

'Very well then. It will do. Can you remember anything about how you got here? I mean apart from Zarath's magicking you awake in the hall last night?'

'I've remembered I was alone on a drifting ship. I cannot remember how I reached land.'

'Or how you got on the ship in the first place?'

'No, illustrious lord,' Mordec lied. 'Not yet. But I think in time it will come back to me.'

'You will tell us when that happens. Can you read and write?'

'Yes, illustrious lord.'

'That's not common among Vikings, is it? Who taught you?'

'My mother. She was a Lombard and grew up in Italy.'

'In Italy? She must be a good cook.'

'She is.'

'Did she teach you to speak Italian?'

Mordec looked up at the ceiling, which was painted with rosy clouds on a blue sky, and was silent for a moment as though testing himself, trying out a few words or phrases in the foreign language.

'Why yes! I remember how to speak Italian, but not when and where I last spoke it.'

'Can you add and divide and multiply numbers?'

Again Mordec looked up at the pink clouds.

'Yes! I can do that too.'

'Do you stammer when you read aloud?'

'No, illustrious lord.'

'How do you get so many colours in you hair?'

'My hair? It does it on its own.'

'Have you travelled much?'

'I don't know, illustrious lord. I think I must have done. Though I can't remember …'

'… Where you've been. Right. Iewan,' he called to the older man attending him, 'the lavender is too strong a scent on the steam. Let's go back to jasmine next time.'

'Yes, my lord,' Iewan replied.

'I'll have a towel now.'

Iewan held the towel and the Lord Alger stepped out of the bath, lightly laying his hand on the extended hand of the young attendant, and the towel was wrapped round him.

'See this, Mordec son of Hauk?' he said. 'This thing called a towel? See how it's made? Like a mown lawn of white grass. It comes from Egypt. Don't know how they do it, but it works wonders. Gets me dry in no time.'

'It is the best towel I have ever seen,' Mordec said.

'Good. Well, off you go then. I'll think about what we can do with you.'

'Do with me?'

The illustrious lord made no answer. His breakfast of many steaming dishes was being carried in by a procession of three pages.

Iewan held the door open for them, and when the last had come through, he gestured to Mordec to leave.

Slate, who had brought him to the door, was waiting just outside it.

'Did he invite you to admire his towel from Egypt?' Slate asked.

'Yes.'

'He was testing your taste. Did you tell him you admired it? Good. Now the Lord Humfrey. This way.

He will have had his all-over douse with cold water and be having his breakfast now. He was particular about just when he would see you.'

Slate sent him in alone to the Lord Humfrey who was standing barefooted but dressed in a dark grey tunic and cloak, in his kitchen, spooning something grey from a bowl into his mouth.

An old woman was stirring the substance in a pot over the fire.

'This,' he told Mordec, 'is called oat porridge. Have you ever seen it before?'

'Yes, illustrious lord.'

'Don't call me that, just "my lord" will do. Do you have it for breakfast at home?'

'Only when we're not feeling well, my lord.'

'Ah, so you understand that it has medicinal qualities?'

'My mother says it soothes an upset stomach.'

'You like it?'

'Oh yes, my lord.' Mordec lied again.

'If you can remember that, you can remember everything. Tell your story to Slate and he'll tell it to me. How you got here and all that.'

'Yes, my lord. Everything I can remember. I'll tell Slate.'

'Can you read, write and reckon?'

'Yes, my lord.'

'Since you are a Viking, I suppose you've been taught how to fight?'

'I have had lessons in fighting, and I most likely have put them to use. I'm a little hazy about that.'

'Ever kill a man?'

'I can't remember. I must have been knocked on the head or something. But I suppose that will come back to me. I'm sure in time I'll remember everything that has happened to me.'

'Can you groom horses?'

'Oh yes. And ride them fast.'

'What else can you do?'

'I can steer a ship, hoist sale, row with long or short oars, and catch fish … And I can harvest honey, boil mead and brew ale. I did that at home. I remember my home and my father and mother clearly. I can't remember why I came away and sailed on a ship alone.'

'Can you obey orders?'

'If—' A frown appeared on the Lord Humfrey's face, distinct enough even to Mordec's eyes, as soon as that one word was uttered. So instead of saying as he'd intended, 'If it's not to do something I'd hate to do,' he said, '*If* my lord will give me an order, I'll do my best to obey it.'

The frown disappeared.

'Your father ever been on a raid in Wales?'

'Oh no, my lord. I don't think he would have done. My father is a meadmaker. He is not a raider.'

Humfrey held out his bowl to the old woman and she refilled it with a ladleful of the oats porridge.

'That is all for now, boy. You may go.'

Slate asked as they hurried away, 'Did he ask you if you are good at obeying orders?'

'I suggested he should test me.'

Slate turned his head to look at Mordec as he said, 'That was a smart answer. You're a clever fellow, aren't you, Mordec son of Hauk?'

'Not so clever to get myself into this pickle.'

Slate turned his gaze up thoughtfully to the overcast sky. 'But clever all the same. Some can be too clever for their own good.'

Mordec was puzzled to understand what he was implying, but had no chance to ask.

'Return to the barn, Mordec. And await orders.'

'Yes, Chief,' Mordec said as he watched Slate hurry away.

servant or slave?

Alger and Humfrey sat at either end of a long table, busy with the government of their corner of Wales.

Slate, the Chief Runner and Executive, sat equidistant between them, noting down their rulings and instructions. His bald pate, reflecting the light from tall windows as he bent his gaze on paper and quill, was dotted here and there with spots of ink left by his fingertips when he rested his head in his hands as he waited for a Lord to come to the point.

The Lords consistently and conscientiously contradicted each other; so Slate, knowing that reconciliation of contradictions is impossible, wrote down what both of them ordained. When the governing session was over, Alger went out by one door and Humfrey by another, and Slate went and did what he thought right, perhaps co-incidentally carrying out an order of Alger here and of Humfrey there, but on the whole making the decisions himself.

The system worked well enough. Runnydale was an orderly little country. The folk believed that the Lords governed them well. Slate was content if everything ran smoothly: if commerce and agriculture continued reliably in all seasons so that the reasonable wants of life were available in the market at competitive prices;

and if there was no serious crime, the cases that came to court, whether of a criminal or civil nature, being seen to be justly dealt with by whichever Lord was on the bench. They sat in judgment turn and turn about once a month at the time of the new moon. Slate was both the Prosecutor and Clerk of the Court.

One question that had been on this morning's government agenda, and had not been resolved by even one of the Lords, was what to do with the new Viking boy. Enslave him? Give him a high salaried position in the castle? Each governor expressed his thoughts as if only to Slate the amanuensis, taking no notice whatsoever of what his co-ruler said.

Alger was for giving Mordec a high position with a salary, since he could read and write.

'Zarath,' he said quietly, 'has given us this boy as a gift. We must make good use of him. He is a Viking, so he would probably be a good warrior. If that was the only consideration, I could put him with the Border Runners or the Coastguard. But it seems he does not see too well. And then, not only is he educated, he has also travelled widely. I would get more from him by employing his mind rather than his muscle.'

Humfrey did not interrupt when Alger spoke. He would gaze into the distance meditatively until Alger was finished, then speak as if Alger had not spoken.

'It was an extraordinary thing that Zarath did, bringing the Viking boy to us.' Humfrey declared emphatically. 'I've been thinking—a gift of gold to Zarath? Or just a raise? I haven't decided which.

Remind me to decide tomorrow, Slate. As for the boy, I cannot make use of him as an armed Runner, nor even as a servant, since his eyesight is weak. I'll put him to work as a teacher, or to assist you, Slate, with the keeping of the records. If he's any good with figures, he could help Tolly the Tally with the accounts. But he's to get no wage. He is a captive and thus he is my slave.'

Slate contributed no opinion or comment. He never did. He might sometimes ask for clarification of an instruction—but very seldom since he was not necessarily going to carry it out anyway—but he never made suggestions. On this subject of the Viking boy, he already had a firm opinion. He feared that his own position as scribe, executive, and keeper of the records, and the power that went with it, would be under threat if either of the Lords had his way.

So Slate decided to help Mordec escape.

Meanwhile, Mordec was at a loose end. He wandered about the palace, the park, the farms, the village (where he attracted curious stares), and along the shore, closely followed by Leif, who chatted to him incessantly without managing to engage his attention. Now and then Mordec would stop to peer closely at some object of interest—a beehive, a book, a sword, all of which set Leif off on a new line of prattle—but generally viewing his new surroundings through a light haze. He hoped to encounter Zarath who might be able to help him get hold of some eyeglasses; not of course by magic, but by taking the practical steps that a man of the world such as Zarath of the East would know how to do. But Zarath was nowhere to be seen.

'Where does Zarath live?' he asked Leif.

'I'll show you. Follow me, Mordec,' Leif said, and he trotted ahead to a tower on a breezy salt-coated corner of the palace, but there was no response to Mordec's knocks with the iron ring on the bleached and abraded door.

When he stopped knocking, Leif took over, and piped 'Zarath, Zarath, my friend that you gave me needs to speak with you!'

But the playful gusts blowing in from the sea carried his words away to make the magician's long underwear, pegged on a line in the jousting court, dance a merry jig.

'Not here!' Leif sad. 'Sorry, Mordec. He's prob'ly in a far off land for a few minutes. He flies faster than an eagle. We'll find him later. He's always back in time for dinner with one of the Lords.'

They returned to the Runners' barn, deserted at that time of day as all the Runners were at work, and Mordec lay down on a bench to think. Hands behind his head, he gazed at the rafters, and Leif did the same on a bench near by. For him, every minute with Mordec was a minute's gain in learning the ways of the Vikings.

'Hmmm,' Mordec hummed.

'Hmmm,' echoed Leif.

'Leif,' Mordec said, 'do you know Slate well?'

'Yes. He takes me to school when he remembers. And he always makes sure I get enough dinner when the Runners would scoff the lot. Believe me, Mordec, he's a good man, even though he's not one of us.'

'What do they teach you at school?' Mordec asked.

'Reading, writing, reckoning, archery, dueling, falconry, Welsh and singing,' Leif reeled off.

'Hmmm,' Mordec hummed again.

'Hmmm,' Leif repeated.

And after a few moments of silence, 'Mordec,' he said.

'Hmm?' Mordec replied.

'Are there many Vikings with the name of Mordec?'

'No. I'm the only one. My mother made it up.'

'Do Viking mothers often make up names?'

'My mother was not always a Viking. She was a Lombard.'

'What's that?'

'The Lombards live in Italy. Years ago my father went raiding on the Middle Sea, and landed in Italy, and met my mother who was called Esther then, and he took her back with him and made her his wife. She became a Viking and changed her name to Estrid. She first wanted to call me Mordecai, but my father thought it sounded too foreign, so she shortened it to Mordec.'

'Have you been on a raid?'

'Yes.'

'Did you take plunder?'

'Yes.'

'What did you take? Children?'

'No, horses.'

Leif let out a long low whistle, and Mordec realized that he was cutting a rather heroic figure—and enjoying it. The kid wasn't such a nuisance after all. And maybe he, Mordec the Raider, did have a duty to school him in Viking ways.

'Were people slain?'

'I nearly was. By being drowned in a bog, but I was saved at the last minute.'

'By other Vikings?'

'Partly by another Viking … 'He stopped abruptly. The Viking who had helped to save him was his best friend Gus. And he and Gus had quarreled on The Good Ship Good just before it was raided and captured by Bjarwulf the Terror of the Seas. Could Gus, he wondered for the first time, have been the snake who'd shut him in the ship's hold and left him there to die? But at once he dismissed the thought as unworthy of a Viking. A Viking did not think such things of a fellow Viking, let alone do such a terrible deed as he had momentarily, meanly, unforgivably, suspected Gus of doing.

He firmly returned his attention to what Leif was saying.

'Have you got brothers and sisters?'

'One brother. He was just a baby when I left to go on a quest through France and Italy.'

'What's his name?'

'Eyrin.'

'And what's your father's name?'

'Hauk son of Hauk. Do you know your father's name?'

'No.'

'Do you remember your father or your mother? Or your first home?'

'No. I was taken by raiders, and taken from them by raiders, and taken from them by raiders, and taken—'

'All right, all right, I get the picture,' Mordec interrupted. 'No need to go on and on.'

But Leif went on.

'There were always nice soft women who held me in their arms, and fed me with spoons, and put clothes on me, and kept me warm, and gave me a smack on the back of my head when I was naughty. Some of them told me stories. Some of them sang to me. One of them laughed a lot. I was passed from one to another until I grew too big to be carried, and then I walked with my hand in the hands of men, and rode on a horse behind a man along with other men riding horses. I remember holding on to the man's belt. Then I remember I was on a ship, and the ship rolled about and I was sick. Then we got into a small boat and landed here, and the men left me here.'

Mordec found this account of Leif's life a little hard to believe. ('They say he's seven. He must be able to remember more than he's telling,' he said to himself.)

But there were more important things needing to be thought about.

'Who is it will decide what to do with me? Will it be the Lords or will it be Slate?'

'I don't know, Mordec.'

'What do you think they'll make me do—whoever it is?'

'They don't make me do anything,' Leif said. 'Except sometimes go to school. Zarath brought you here to be my friend. I don't think they'll make you do anything but be my friend. I don't think Zarath would like it if they made you do something else.'

But Mordec doubted he'd be left to do nothing but keep the little boy company. They wouldn't be feeding him for nothing. It wasn't the way of the world. The Lords might try to sell him. If that didn't work—or until some buyer turned up—they'd be sure to make him earn his keep. He wondered what labor they'd put him to.

If only he could persuade them to demand ransom for him! If they got a message to any Vikings anywhere in England—or on a raid into Wales—that they were holding Mordec son of Hauk and would hand him over for a sum in gold, it would get back to his father … who'd come with fearless fighters to get him, more likely bearing arms than ransom. 'And of course,' he realized, 'that's exactly why they won't do it.'

Perhaps he could persuade them to let him go on the grounds that if they didn't, Viking raiders might come looking for him.

'Could Slate arrange for me to speak to the Lords? And if he could, do you think he would?'

'I don't know, Mordec.'

'Do travelers often pass through Runnydale? Raiders perhaps? Or traders?'

'Not often. Raiders or traders must have brought me here. Perhaps they traded me. Perhaps they sold me to the Lords.'

'Do Runnydale people themselves go raiding?'

'I've never heard of anyone from here going on a raid.'

'Do they go to war? Do they try and conquer other people?'

'They just live here and farm and make things like shoes and … and … cloaks and … and …' He looked about the barn for something that could be made. '… harps and … jugs. And they sell them in the market.'

'Do they sail to other lands? Where are their ships?'

'They only have small boats. They row them about the bay and catch fish. You aren't thinking of going away from here, are you, Mordec? Please don't leave me. It's nice here. You'll like it.'

'I must get back to my country.'

'Then you'll take me with you? Don't forget I'm a Viking too.'

'Come, little nuisance, I'll teach you a Viking game,' Mordec said. 'It's called hnefatafl.'

First they had to find twenty-four black stones, twelve white stones, and one bigger stone called the King. Then Mordec led the way to the shore, and drew a 'board' in the sand: a square of eleven squares by eleven squares. The twenty-four black stones were arranged in groups of six on each side, the King in the middle on a square called the Throne, the white stones protecting him. The black stones must try to capture the King, Mordec explained, by surrounding him on four sides. The King must try to escape by reaching one of the four corners of the board.

Leif proved to be very good at the game once he'd got the hang of it. When he'd beaten Mordec for the fourth time, twice taking the side of the black attackers and twice the side of the King, Mordec told him he'd had enough and anyway it was time for dinner.

Later that night, unable to sleep, Mordec wandered out of the barn to walk along the edge of the sea. The moon lit his way. There was a chance, he hoped, that the tide would bring The Good Ship Good back to the shore. If it did, he wanted to escape on it before anyone else saw it. He'd heard there was a Coastguard, but not seen it.

If the chance came, should he take Leif with him or not? Well, he suggested to himself, if the boy was with him when the moment came, yes. He could use another pair of hands on the ship. But if it was night, and getting the boy meant rousing him from sleep and risking being heard by others in the barn, he would rather slip away and manage the ship on his own.

No ship was in sight. He came across a fisherman's rowing-boat and had an impulse to steal it and row away—but where to? How long, how far could he keep rowing, and without even having a destination in mind? Another shore? If inhabited, it was unlikely to be better than Runnydale. If uninhabited, he would not have improved his lot.

Besides, what if he were caught by the Coastguard? If they caught him on The Good Ship Good, he would be brought back, but he would not have done anything wrong. But if he were to be overtaken in a stolen fishing-boat, he would have to face trial and punishment, and he didn't want to go through that again.

Starting back towards the palace, he noticed there was a light in the top of the tower where Zarath lived.

'He might be awake,' Mordec thought. 'I could try knocking gently on his door.'

zarath and the birds

Mordec knocked gently with the iron knocker, then a little harder, and finally hard on the door of the tower, and was rewarded at last by hearing a bolt being drawn. The door opened a crack.

'Who's there?' a voice demanded. 'What do you want?'

'Mordec the Viking. I want to talk to Zarath, please.'

'You'd better come in.'

The door opened a little wider, and Mordec stepped into a dim space lit only by a pale green light emitted by a hierarchy of glowworms, one on each step of a staircase which followed the circular wall in a long spiral to the top of the tower.

'Follow me,' the Magician said—for it was he—as he started up the stairs. 'Don't tread on my worms.'

Near the top of the tower, they passed through an open door into a room crowded with things. Oil lamps lit it, and the moonlight streaming in through windows on three sides.

Now Mordec could see that the tall form of Zarath was dressed in a long dark green gown. A matching cap covered his hair, ears, forehead and eyebrows. He sank into a nest of cushions on an intricately carved armchair. He did not invite Mordec to be seated, or even point to one of the many chairs in the room. There were small ones piled on top of each other, and a few large ones on which boxes, wands, musical instruments, plates, goblets, cloaks, hats, and horned animal heads were stacked haphazardly. The room was lighted and warmed by a low-burning fire of glowing logs in a stone fireplace. Mordec stood and was about to speak when the Magician said, 'Don't mention it.'

For a moment Mordec wondered if his thoughts had been read; if Zarath really did have magical powers and knew that he had come to ask for help with what would in fact be a secret plot, and Zarath was warning him not even to speak of it. But he dismissed the absurd notion.

'Mention what?' he asked in a polite tone.

'You were going to thank me for saving you from whatever hardships tossed you onto this shore, for transporting you into this pleasant land of Runnydale, and making you famous among the people.'

'Well …'

Mordec was about to say 'Well, no,' when he thought better of it. He had come to ask the Magician to do him a favor. It would be sensible to flatter him a little.

'Yes, as a matter of fact I was,' Mordec said in a tone of delighted surprise. 'However did you know that?'

'Ah!' Zarath said, smiling. 'I can see a little way into other minds. It's a part of my talent.'

'Your talent?' Mordec said. 'Your genius, I would say.'

'And I would not blame you. But I am not a man who needs gratitude and applause to support my self-confidence. See, I wave away your thanks.' And he waved his right hand about above his head.

'Well, yes, thanks … I mean … thanks again. And—er—there's something else I came to say. To ask you.'

'Oh, I know. But go ahead and ask.'

'Have you ever heard of a Troll named Julius?'

For a brief moment Zarath looked startled. ('He hadn't expected that,' Mordec thought.) But then the Magician gave a short laugh and what he said in reply was more than Mordec could have expected.

'Heard of him? I know him well. He's what I might call my agent. He it is who finds out where I am needed and notifies clients of my fees and arranges the means to get me there.'

'You get messages to him and from him?'

'Yes.'

'May I ask how?' Mordec said, knowing how, but intending to flatter the great man again.

'No,' Zarath said. 'I never tell how I do my magic.'

'Could you get a message to him from me?'

'I could, yes. The question should not be could I, but would I.'

'Would you get a message to him to let my father and mother know that I am here? Julius the Troll knows me, he knows where we live—'

'I will not help you escape from Runnydale, dear boy. I am loyal to those who employ me. The Lords Alger and Humfrey want to keep you here.'

'But you magicked me here to be a friend for Leif. The Lords didn't ask for me. I can take Leif with me.'

'I'll do nothing to help you leave as long as the Lords want you to stay. If you can talk them into letting you go, then I'll help you.'

Mordec could tell that Zarath would remain firm on this point.

'I see. Then let me ask for something else.'

'The Granting,' Zarath said, 'when I make a few wishes come true, takes place in Runnydale only once a year.'

Mordec ignored the objection. He went on: 'Would you ask Julius to let my father and mother know that I am alive and well—without saying where I am?'

'If any message from you to Julius is sent by me, he'll know where you are. Now don't misunderstand me. I believe he is honourable. After all, I trust him with my professional life. But when it comes to letting anxious parents know where their lost son may be found, he just might decide to spill the beans.'

Mordec nodded slowly. 'No chance of that then.'

'Sorry, but no. I like you, Mordec. I would help you if it was the ethical thing for me to do. But, I regret to have to say, it is not.'

Mordec nodded. 'I'll say good-night to you then,' he said affably, making for the door.

He had started down the spiraling stairs, feeling for each step since the glow worms did not cast a bright enough light to be more than a very little help to his myopic eyes, when Zarath called after him, 'Don't tread on my worms!'

'I won't,' Mordec called back. And stopped still.

He stood listening intently.

He had heard a low riffling sound coming from somewhere over his head.

'The pigeons! He keeps them here in the top of the tower.'

He smiled, and called again, 'I'll be very careful!'

Zarath listened to the descending footsteps and the loud clank of the front door when it shut behind his departing guest.

'A good-natured fellow,' he said aloud to himself. 'Well brought up. Well mannered for a Viking. Knows not to argue with his betters. He'll settle down. And one day, perhaps, the Lords will let him go. In any case, my stock of birds is running low and Julius hasn't yet found a way to send me more.'

Mordec pulled the front door closed by means of its knocker. No sooner was it firmly shut than a voice spoke out of the darkness, rebuking him, at the same time as something soft pressed against his back, and he felt himself trapped as if by a very large cushion.

'Didn't you hear me?' the voice said close to his ear, 'I said don't shut it. I want to go in.'

'I didn't hear you say that,' Mordec said, edging himself away from the space between the owner of the voice and the door.

He now saw by the moon's light the person with whom he was conversing. It was the very large lady who had been sitting with Alger and Humfrey the night he had woken to a thunder of applause in this strange land.

'Ah, now I know you!' she exclaimed. 'You came to woo me when I was travelling through Italy on the way to England. You and a taller one with lovely yellow hair. I liked him better. Where's he got to now?'

The Princess Starling! Mordec recalled vividly how he and Gus and Hengist had been marshaled by two armed men into a caravan where the ample Princess had sat on many cushions, surrounded by other ladies.

'What was his name?' she demanded now.

'Gus son of Hakon,' Mordec said very softly, more to himself than to his questioner. Again that thought rose unbidden and unwelcome. Had it been Gus, could it have been Gus, who …

'Speak up,' the Princess said. 'Can't hear you. Never mind. Off you go. You are the wrong one.'

She started to knock on the door very hard many times with the iron knocker, and as the door was opened for her to enter, Mordec hurried away. He avoided the Runners on patrol, whose marching he could hear approaching, by hiding in the dark recesses of the palace walls, in shrubberies, and behind the stout trunks of trees until the groups of three or four men had passed by.

Leif slept on in 'their' corner of the barn, unaware that Mordec had gone away and returned, and undisturbed by the racket the Runners made as they drank, talked, laughed, and played a gambling game using shells for tokens. Mordec sat beside Leif, far from the fire, writing by the light of a candle stub, on two narrow strips of cloth he had torn from the hem of a white tunic someone had left lying about, using a fish bone as a pen. He had pricked his finger with the fish bone and his ink was his own blood. Peering closely, hardly seeing what he was doing (though he had never worn his glasses for reading and writing) he wrote the same message on each piece of cloth in tiny letters: in wales homing mordec.

Then he lay down on the straw beside Leif, and slept.

In the morning, while Leif was at school, he returned to Zarath's tower and watched it from behind a row of gooseberry bushes. There he waited patiently while the sun rose, bright but not warm to the top of the sky. At last Zarath emerged, pulled his front door firmly closed, and set off walking at a leisurely pace. Mordec waited until he was out of sight, made sure as best he could that nobody was watching him from the gardens or the palace windows, and went to find a way into the tower.

It was surprisingly easy. A window not far above the ground, letting light onto the stairs, had only one bar down its middle. Mordec pulled himself up by it onto the sill, and squeezed past it. Once inside he stood still a moment, listening. There was no sound of voices or anyone moving about, only, as last night, that faint riffling sound, and now and then a low deep coo.

He raced up the stairs to find a closed door at the top. A flimsy thing, it was not locked, nor even firmly closed. He pushed it open, stepped into a round room, and closed the door softly. And there they were: pigeons. Homing pigeons, for sure. What else what would Zarath keep them for? He could see them well enough, by the sunlight coming in through many holes in the shutters over the wide window and shining directly on the wall where they were nested. From what Zarath had said about Julius being his agent, Mordec reasoned that at least some of these must fly home to the Troll. He took one firmly in his hand, held it lightly upside down between his knees and tied his message to one of its legs. Then he put the bird back in its nest and did the same with the other. Finally he lifted the wooden shutter and launched the birds quickly one after the other into the air. He watched the two blurred blots rising, circling, and—to his great relief—starting north-east-ward. 'They will get there,' he told himself. 'My luck has turned.'

Very quietly he left the room, closed the door, and stood listening for a moment or two before creeping down the stairs. He was out of the low window and moving rapidly away from the tower when he dimly saw and was seen by a pair of Runners who were strolling round the palace on guard duty. He smiled and waved at them cheerfully and they nodded to him.

The pigeons were caught in flight by a pair of Slate's falcons, launched by his falconer as always when pigeons flew out of the top of the tower unless he was told by his employer that Zarath had been granted permission to send a message. The falconer brought Mordec's notes to Slate, who read them and dropped

them on the fire in his dining-room. He wanted no
Viking rescue party coming here. The sooner Mordec
was sent on his way, the better.

escape

Next morning, when Mordec was again alone in the barn, he sat looking up at the rafters, at the shapes hanging there which he had been told were smoked hams and musical instruments. His short-sighted eyes moved to a shelf where, he knew, were stored loaves of coarse bread—and which he realized he wanted a few bites of right now. Leif had been hauled off to school by Slate before he could charm some breakfast delicacies out of a soft-hearted cook.

'This sort of bread,' he thought, as he went to get one down, 'would taste and even feel much the same when it got stale. It could last for days.'

He broke off a piece from a loaf and began to chew it with some force.

'Too many would be a burden at the start, when I'll need to move fast.'

He looked at the loaves, then up to where the hams hung, then at the loaves again. Now was the time to seize what he wanted and start his escape. Yet he hesitated. The Runners, especially Slate and Flint, had been good to him. 'I'll be thanking them by stealing their food!' he found himself thinking. And immediately another thought followed: 'It's absurd for a Viking to have scruples about taking what he wants.

Vikings plunder. It's what we do. I guess the Lombard side of me is quarreling with the Viking side.'

And he was just about to let the Viking side win, reach out and grab a few loaves, and was already thinking about where he could hide them along with a ham or two while he went looking for a sack to carry them in, when he fuzzily perceived the recognizable figure of the head Runner coming through the big open door, propelling Leif before him.

'He took me to school and then he fetched me out of it again.' Leif called out to Mordec. 'In the middle of a history lesson. But I don't mind.'

Slate let go of the boy, strode up to Mordec and looked into his eyes. Mordec felt guilty, his face grew hot. But without a word, Slate turned his gaze to the shelves of bread, took down four loaves, and pushed them into Mordec's arms.

Mordec opened his mouth to ask why, but had his answer before he'd uttered a word.

'For the journey,' Slate said. Then out of a closet reserved to him alone, he brought a sack and a knife. He opened the sack and held it out to Mordec, who was still gaping at him. Slate nodded to indicate that the loaves should go into the sack. Mordec obediently dropped them in.

'Here, hold this,' Slate ordered.

Mordec held the sack and watched Slate climb on a bench and cut down a ham, and then another and another, and put them in with the loaves.

'I'm putting the knife in too,' Slate said. 'You'll need it. Now listen carefully. First, don't dawdle. In three days from now snow will begin to cover the peak and it will quickly become impossible for anyone to get over it. Next, …'

Mordec listened attentively to Slate's plan. Slate himself would escort him to the border and show him the start of the hidden path through the rocky mountain.

Then he asked Slate—Chief Runner, head of the Border Guards and all other forces of law and order in Runnydale—why he was helping him.

'I'll tell you when I leave you at the border,' Slate said. 'Now hide all this under the straw near the door, and as soon as the men have eaten their lunch and gone to play ball, I'll come and fetch you. And tell the kid to keep his mouth shut. He's a natterer. He can natter again when you're both safely over the mountain.'

So Leif was to come too on the hazardous journey to England. 'Well,' Mordec thought, 'a second pair of hands is always useful, and besides, he is a Viking.' And at once he corrected the thought. 'He's a Viking, and besides, a second pair of hands is always useful.'

'You'll need his eyes too,' Slate said. 'Especially on the rocky mountain where the secret trail is narrow and hard to see with the best of sight.'

'Could everyone round here read minds?' Mordec wondered.

No one challenged Chief Runner Slate as he marched the two Viking boys, bearing sacks of something to carry out a job of some sort, through the palace grounds, through a gate in the back wall, through a wood of oak and elm, across a heath, to the foot of the mountains that marked the eastern border of Runnydale.

'Here, between these two giant rocks, the path begins. See? It will be fairly easy at first. Then it will get steep and narrow and hard, but it's the only way unless you're a trained rock-climber. Get going now to cover as much distance as you can before dark. *And whatever happens, don't come back,*' Slate instructed Mordec.

Mordec dropped his sack to the ground and faced the Chief Runner.

'Before I go, I want to know why. Why you are doing this—helping me escape. You said you would tell me …'

'You will understand,' Slate said. 'One of these days your people will come to Runnydale, either as traders or raiders. I don't want them to think that we kept you either as a slave or a servant. I want them to know that you were shipwrecked on our shore, and I helped you on your way back home.'

Mordec wished he could see Slate's eyes clearly to help him judge if the man spoke sincerely, but without bringing his face within a few inches of Slate's, he couldn't do that. Instead he thought about what Slate had said for a moment or two.

'Yes, that makes sense,' he said. 'What will you tell the Rulers?'

'That I brought you here to do a job—clear stones from the path across the heath—and while I was called away briefly to see to some emergency, you escaped. I will point out that without guidance you would probably not find the path up the mountain, and would most likely perish. You won't, of course,' he added hastily. 'Stay on the path and you'll be safe. Going down will be easier.'

He warned of a few hazards. He wanted them to travel far.

'Once you are over the peak you are out of Runnydale. What you do after that is up to you. Eastward, beyond more mountains, lies England. Southward—a long way south—lies the biggest trading port of Wales. You'll look after the child, won't you?'

'*I'll* look after *him*,' Leif said. 'He can't see properly.'

'I wish you both good fortune,' Slate said. 'Go carefully and farewell.'

He turned abruptly and hurried off. Mordec called 'Farewell and thank you!' after him, and Leif echoed 'Farewell and thank you!', and Slate raised a hand and dropped it without turning or slackening his pace.

He was soon out of Leif's sight.

'He waved,' he told Mordec.

'He's a good man,' Mordec said.

'A good man,' Leif agreed.

Mordec soon found that Leif, far from being a drag on his progress, was as indispensable to it as Leif himself had predicted. He walked ahead of Mordec and *saw* the way.

The path Slate had set them on was hard to discern even to Leif's keen eyes. And no easy climb was it, over the towering rock-mountain that shut Runnydale off from the rest of Wales. At some points it was obscured by heaps of small stones, at others it forced the travellers to drag themselves and their baggage under, or struggle over, formidable barriers of boulders.

Mordec bore a heavy sack filled with loaves and hams, and Leif a lighter one with one more loaf and one more ham in it. They went as far as they could before darkness made further advance too perilous to attempt. Then they sheltered under an overhang, leant their backs against the wall of stone, and Mordec doled out their equal rations of bread and meat.

There was no lack of water. The sound of dripping was in their ears continuously, and the sound of streams often. They stepped over narrow rivulets and passed behind waterfalls.

And then, before the morning dawned, it began to rain.

And rain, and rain. A thunderstorm broke before dawn, the roar seeming to Mordec to start right over his head before rolling away into a great distance; and the fork lightening, which illumined the black rocks of the mountain and the silver rain brilliantly for a few seconds, several times seemed to try reaching in to strike him or the sleeping form of Leif—who amazingly slept through the enormous noise.

He had found a ledge just wide and long enough to support his curled up body, and using his sack as a pillow, he slept peacefully. Mordec had spread his own cloak—a blue one, gifted to him by one of the Runners—over his young companion, though he himself shivered in his worn tunic.

Before dawn the storm subsided, but the rain continued. The dark clouds kept the day from becoming much brighter than the night had been.

'Is it still night?' was the first thing Leif said on opening his eyes.

'Not by name.' Mordec said. 'It may clear a bit later. As soon as you're sure you can see the path well enough, we'll go on. First, we'll have breakfast.'

'I've never known a day so dim,' Leif said.

'Oh this isn't a dark day compared to what it's like at home this time of year,' Mordec informed him as he bit into a slice of ham wrapped in dank bread. The prevailing moisture had got through the sack and the loaves had sponged it up.

'It's dark all day?'

'It's dark all season. We have a night that lasts for months. But in summer we have hardly any night at all.'

'Tell me more about home.'

'Look!' Mordec pointed, rising to his feet. 'There's a break in the clouds. Let's see if we can reach the top.'

They made slow progress for the first hour or two. Then suddenly the sun came out. Leif shouted, 'The sun! Mordec, the sun! I can see now. Come on.' And he began to walk faster.

'Don't go too far ahead,' Mordec called. 'If I lose sight of you I could fall off the mountain!'

'The sun dried their clothes.' Looking up, Leif saw the summit they were aiming for. It was white with snow, glistening in the sunlight.

They reached it in the early afternoon. The snow was thin, but under it were holes covered with ice, impossible to see. Their boots cracked the ice, and more than once they found themselves standing with one leg in an earth-bucket of bitingly cold water as they traversed a flat oval ringed with white rocks—

'Like a pie, it's like a huge pie.' Leif said. 'Sometimes the Rulers sent us pies when they had too many.'

'What was in them?' Mordec asked.

'Usually eel. Sometimes apple. Once one of the pies had pigeon inside it, and when I told Zarath he was angry. He said the pigeon was a special bird that carried messages for him.'

'Oh. He said that did he?' Mordec murmured thoughtfully.

'He wanted to know who had shot it down, and whether it had had anything tied to its leg, but no one owned up. I think it was Flint who shot it, but I didn't say so to Zarath. I asked Flint if he did it, and all he said was that if there was anything tied to that bird's leg, it was lost and gone.'

They had now come to the edge of the 'pie', and they peered between the white rocks. Mordec expected to see a valley below, or a wide plain of green fields stretching out to the horizon. To his disappointment all he saw was fog. Here they were high on the mountain with the sun beating down on their heads, and down there—starting a little further than he could reach—was a sea of grey fog.

'We can't go down. We must wait for the fog to clear.'

Slate had assured them that going down would not be hard, that the slope was quite easy and all they had to do was avoid the ravines and the streams in spate.

They cleared snow from a flat rock, sat and ate. And the dark came, and another dawn, and the sea of fog was still there.

Mordec kept Leif entranced with the tale of how he had found a small ship which he had named Foal of the Foam, and had sailed in it along with the big ships to raid England, and all that had happened to him there.

'If the fog's still here tomorrow, 'I'll tell you what happened to me in Italy. Now we'll eat and try to sleep.'

Leif ate quietly for a while, thinking over what he had heard. Then he said, 'Mordec?'

'Hm?'

'There's a name that I know. I don't know why I remember it. Maybe you know someone who has that name.'

'Maybe. What is it?'

'Harry? Something like that. Is it a Viking name?'

'I haven't heard of a Viking named Harry, but it could be a Viking name.'

'I think someone named Harry carried me once. Maybe he was the Viking who gave me away.'

'If we ever get back home,' Mordec said, 'I'll try to find that Harry. If he did you wrong—'

'Like that Viking boy Kol son of Knefrod did to you.'

'Like certain Vikings did to me …' Mordec said grimly. As the days had gone by, he had become ever more, though still reluctantly, sure that it was Gus who had confined him in the hold of The Good Ship Good when Bjarwulf's men had set it on fire.

'Only Kol was never brought before the Thing to be judged, was he? But we'll bring Harry before the Thing if he gave me away.'

'Or sold you.'

'Or sold me. And he'll be made my bondsman for the rest of his life!' Leif said, happy to show that he was learning well what Mordec taught him about how things were done 'at home'.

captain anwid

What had happened to the ship which had borne Mordec to this corner of Wales?

She had been carried out and in again to the shallows as the tide went out and in on the night when everyone was distracted by the Granting. But the next day a strong current took her far out and she did not drift in again. No Runnydale fishermen saw her. Nor the keen-eyed Coast Guard. In the first days of his captivity, Mordec had come to the beach often to watch for her, but by the fourth day had given up hope that she would return.

Someone else was looking for her: her captain, Anwid, daughter of the Earl of Felldown.

'Father, I'm off again' Anwid said.

Her father looked up from his breakfast of red pig trotters and a big blue boiled penguin egg. 'Eh?' he said. 'To sea again? Thought your ship had been scuttled by pirates.'

'They set fire to her,' Anwid said. 'But I think there may have been someone on board, and perhaps the fire was put out, and perhaps she is still out there somewhere. I'm going to look for her.'

'Got hold of another ship?'

'I'll travel overland. On foot.'

'Oh? Well, you always know what you're doing, my dear. If anyone can find a ship by scouring the land, you're the gel to do it.'

'I'm taking what's left of my crew with me.'

'The plain gels. The very tall thin one with red hair and freckles. And the short fat one. And the one who sniffs.'

'I'd no idea you'd noticed so much about them. Actually, some of them are the hardiest I ever had, and they're all good fighters. Especially the very tall thin one with red hair.'

'They'll need to be.'

'I need something from you, Father.'

'Anything that's in my power to give you is yours except my favorite horse, my sword and my estates—which will be yours anyway, in time.'

'All I want is a letter.'

'To whom?'

'To all the earls, kings, queens and princes, of all the earldoms, kingdoms, queendoms and princedoms throughout England. But just one letter will do. I'll show it and keep it.'

'What do you want me to say?'

'Tell them that I, the bearer of the letter, am your daughter. Ask them to help me in the reasonable ways I shall request.'

'I don't know 'em all.'

'Two letters then. One to those you know and one to those you don't.'

This is one of the letters he wrote, to be shown to those he knew. He listed their names.

Hello old dear,
  This is my gel Anwid.
  She is a good sort.
  Be kind to her dearheart.
  But what is past is past. Don't tell her a thing.
  And may you stay safe from the fury of the Northmen.
Ever your
Bummy

And this is the other letter, the one to be shown to strangers.

Fellow-country-man or lady, majesty, highness, or esquire,
  I, Botham Cogg, Earl of Felldown, request your kind reception of my daughter Anwid, bearer of this letter.
  In anticipation of good chance to return favor to you or yours.
Felldown

'Those will do nicely,' Anwid said.

She embraced him fondly. 'I'll be back,' she said.

'And then you will stay long enough to marry and bear my grandsons?'

'Goes without saying,' she assured him.

hunters of the seas

Captain Bjarwulf was bored, bored, bored. He played hnefatafl or Eyes and Nose with Pelf late into the night (and Pelf let him win every second game). From dawn to dark the captain paced the deck, or stood beside the lookout (the best of whom was the keen-eyed Delfinola), or beside Hauk who was almost always looking out as they dared the winter sea between France and England. Or he drank and ate with Hakon and Gus, and paced the deck. He had never in all his life—and he had started pirating with his dad when he was four—had such a dull voyage. When a ship was sighted he longed to plunder it with a longing like that of a thirsty man for water.

He amused himself by imagining how his fast ship would gain on the other; how his grappling-hooks would grab the timbers and hold the vessel fast; how his men would leap on her, the swords flash, the spears find their mark, and then ... the opening of the hold, the first view of the cargo, Pelf assessing it with his experienced eye ... But he kept his promise to Hauk and sailed steadily on, southward to the region of the channel where he had plundered The Good Ship Good.

Delfinola would know The Good Ship Good, her own home on the seas for many a year, if she only glimpsed her even through rain or mist or fog or snow. And Bjarwulf himself would know her when he saw her: a broad, shallow-bottomed tub, with a raised deck fore and aft, she was like no other ship known to the ports. She never carried anything of real value, and he had only raided it that time as an easy practice raid for his new young cadet pirates.

He had let Captain Anwid of The Good Ship Good gamble at Eyes and Nose for her girls, since he'd heard there was no market for girl slaves that season so it didn't matter much if he lost some of them. But on the voyage home from England he had heard of a sudden demand for them among the Moors of Andalus. He had not needed to take the selected beauties all the way to southern Spain himself, but had transferred them, in exchange for marbles and leathers and pistachios, to the high-pooped craft of an earless Moorish captain off the coast of northern France—while the prentice boys, who had thought the girls were theirs to keep, had grumbled loudly, 'Aah! No-o-o!', making Bjarwulf and Pelf guffaw.

Sometimes the captains of the ships that came in sight recognized the Serpent King for the pirate ship, the menace of the seas, that it was, and piled on sail and took up more oars and fled as fast as wind and muscle would let them. Then Bjarwulf would sigh and smile, feeling regret mingled with satisfaction: regret that he could not pursue them, satisfaction that he was so famously feared.

Day and night the sea was boisterous though not stormy. Rain clouds gathered but thinned, gathered again and thinned again, keeping the sun screened, the moon veiled, the stars often invisible. Steady navigation was made possible by the blotch of a sun and the faint coastline of England appearing now and then far to their right in the winter daylight.

Sometimes Delfinola would sing into the wind, her long white hair blowing about her head, her notes and words now loud now soft as the gusts seized and dropped them.

Of the songs she sang, this was the one she liked best and delivered with the most dramatic power:

My love is tossed
Upon the wave
If he be lost
No earthly grave
Will hold his bones upon the shore,
Nor will my arms, for evermore.

A doodle-doo, a doodle-day,
I watched my true love sail away.

Though love I may
My sailor man
He will not stay
With me on land
He leaves me lone upon the shore,
Nor will return, for evermore.

A doodle-doo, a doodle day,
I watched my true love sail away.

I'll find a land man
now to wed
Who'll proudly hand me
To his bed.
I'll stand no more upon the shore
Wailing lost love for evermore.

A doodle-doo, a doodle-day,
I watched my true love sail away.

So fare thee well my darling boy
And though I am forsaken
I'll not grow fat for lack of joy
But breakfasting on bacon.

The words always brought tears to the eyes of Pelf, and even Bjarwulf swallowed hard each time the chorus rang out. The tune haunted the crew. One of them, Lars, hummed or whistled the tune incessantly while he swabbed the deck and took his turn at the rudder.

'She's worth every penny, my wife,' Pelf often confided to his pillow before he slept and dreamed his golden dreams.

the castle of yggdrasil

Anwid and her intrepid crew were making progress down the east coast of England, walking from dawn to dusk along cliffs and beaches, spending the cold nights rolled up in furs in the great halls of firelit castles.

Anwid boasted that she could sleep with one eye open to watch over her girls. The least creak of a door, or clink of armour at the change of the watch, sprang both her eyelids open. Her very nerves were trained to keep her true to her stalwart guardianship—though truth to tell, the knights and servants of the castles, after crowding the ramparts when first they were hailed by the voice of a lady, seemed to lose interest after a short stare at the younger visitors.

The letter she bore from her father assured her of hospitality for herself and her twenty plain but serviceable maidens. Their hosts either remembered 'Bummy' well and asked after him affectionately, or sent their compliments to the noble Earl of Felldown whom they had not had the honour of meeting yet in person.

And the mariners were sumptuously fed on venison dressed in red currents that shone in the firelight like a thousand round rubies; the legs of sheep steeped in yellow ale and rolled in the grey spikes of fragrant rosemary; stews of mixed meats and roots flavored with precious green pepper; and round white bread-loaves with golden crusts made of thrice-sifted barley flour.

'So you seek your ship along the coast? You look close at wreckage strewn among the rocks? You search deep into the mouths of the rivers? Pray tell us the tale of how you lost her,' the princes and lords and ladies would ask their guests as they dined at the long table.

And Anwid would tell her tale: her ship raided by Viking pirates, set alight and adrift, her crew divided, some taken prisoner and possibly enslaved, the remnant landed with her on the coast of England near her home.

At the end of the fifth day, as dusk was about to fall in the middle of the afternoon, Anwid stood on the peak of a small hill and scanned the landscape for a habitation. One of her keener-eyed sailors, strong, wiry, red-haired Dellibeth, came and stood beside her, and at once spotted a raised pennant whipping about in the chill wind a mile or so to the south-southeast.

They reached the castle before dark, and Anwid hailed the watch on the battlements—two men in chainmail and high-arched helmets, with visors raised.

'We come in peace,' she called. 'We beg a night's lodging.'

To her surprise a woman answered, appearing suddenly between the two knights.

'And who are you, pray?' She called.

'Anwid, daughter of Earl Felldown, and also known as Captain Cogg of The Good Ship Good which is perhaps wrecked along the shore, I and my crew.'

She was surprised again by the next question.

'Are you Christians?' the lady asked very distinctly, leaning over the wall of the watch-tower, her long blue sleeves dangling half-way to the moat.

'Well, yes,' Anwid replied. 'Sort of. I suppose. I mean yes, but not specially. Do we have to be—to be let in and lodged?'

Now a bearded man in a blue cloth hat and dark blue robe appeared beside the lady.

'How Christian would you say you are?' he called. 'On a scale of one to ten?'

'Mmmm—about … five?' Anwid called back.

'Five,' the man repeated dubiously.

'Four and a half?' Anwid tried, though unsure whether to raise or lower ther estimate.

'All right then,' the lady called. 'You can come in.'

The drawbridge was lowered with a loud rattling of chairs, and the portcullis raised. Anwid led her girls in a straight line over the moat and through an arch of stone towards the castle yard. Feeling that she was walking on something uneven, she looked down to find a net beneath her feet—a net that could suddenly be pulled up to enclose intruders and hoist them to the roof. She looked up and saw that the curved roof was studded with iron spikes. This was an entrance designed to destroy invading enemies. She reached her right arm across her body and gripped the hilt of her sword.

In the yard she found armoured guards standing at intervals along the enclosing walls, spears lowered and pointed towards her and her crew. But none stood close to her and none moved towards her. She did not feel threatened. She was a stranger and therefore not to be wholly trusted, but she was not reckoned to be an immediate threat.

A yellow liveried, unarmed young page bowed and conducted them into a very long, very wide, very high, wood-paneled hall.

At one end, on a raised platform, behind a dining table, stood a Viking ship. At the other, the wall was covered from top to bottom and from side to side with a tapestry picturing a tree.

The man and woman who had spoken to them from the ramparts now came forward to greet them graciously. The man had a sword hung on his left hip, its hilt studded with polished stones, opaque but gleaming; some an intense blue which Anwid named to herself as 'lapis lazuli', and some black. 'Jet,' Anwid thought. And the woman wore necklaces of the same blue and black stones.

'My name is Askr,' the man said. 'And this lady is my wife, Embla. We are Vikings. At least, *she* is a Viking, born and bred. I *became* a Viking. It was the condition on which she agreed to marry me,' he explained, going slightly red in the face. 'Come and sit here on my right. My wife sits always on my left. My taster sits under the table.'

Space was made for Anwid. Diners already seated and eating smiled and nodded to her as they shuffled along the bench to make room for her. She smiled and nodded back, and sat down carefully, looking down to see if her feet were in danger of encountering the taster.

'Oh, he's not really there,' Askr said. 'I was only joking. The taster sits in the doorway and tastes every dish as it comes out of the kitchen. Help yourself to the dishes that take your fancy. They're all fish. Different fish. Cooked different ways, but only Viking ways. We have a Viking cook. I noticed you looked at our ship and our tree. Do you know what sort of ship it is, and the name of the tree?'

'I know the ship is a Viking ship. The Vikings make the best ships in the world.'

'Yes. It is the very ship in which my beautiful wife sailed to these shores. And the tree is the holy tree of the Vikings, Yggdrasil. This castle is named Yggdrasil in honour of the tree.'

'Ah,' Anwid said, enjoying her fish but chewing carefully and being reluctant to talk, fearing she might swallow a bone. The taste was delicious, but the bones were many. She knifed a large piece from a new dish that had appeared before her, and put a strip in her mouth. There were no bones in this one but it did not taste delicious. She lifted another piece on the point of her knife and sniffed it. It smelt like—pee.

'That's a special Viking delicacy,' Askr whispered near her ear. 'We call it pee-shark.'

'The roots of Yggdrasil,' the lady Embla was intoning in a rapt voice, 'clasp the whole earth, and its branches hold up the sky.'

'Mmmm-*hmmm!*' said Anwid, trying to make the sound full of polite appreciation of the marvels described to her, while she kept her lips closed and tried to swallow the pee-shark.

'Askr and Embla were the first mortal man and the first mortal woman,' Askr said.

Anwid dipped her head to acknowledge that she had taken in this new information.

'These stones,' Embla said, touching her necklaces, are the colours sacred to Odin, black and blue.'

'Beautiful!' Anwid said.

'We will now be entertained by a singer who will sing a Viking song about Yggdrasil,' Embla announced, and clapped three times.

A boy carrying a lyre walked to the middle of the hall, sat on a low stool, and sang in a clear high voice:

I Odin hung on a windy tree
nine nights long,
wounded with a spear in my side,
I sacrificed myself to Odin,
myself to myself,
on that gallows tree whose roots run
too deep for any man to know where
and whose branches reach
too high for any man
to know where.

Having safely swallowed her last bite of fish, Anwid said, 'What an amazing song—and how beautifully the singer sang.'

She clapped her hands loudly and rapidly, and her girls, seated at a table further down the hall, followed her lead and clapped heartily too.

'Jolly good, bravo!' Anwid called out. Then, turning to her hosts, she said, 'But I am puzzled by the words of the song. I mean—do the Vikings—sorry, I mean do *you* Vikings believe—no, I mean, do you Vikings *know* that Odin "sacrificed himself to himself"?'

'Yes, good lady,' Embla replied. 'It is one of the points on which our religion finds an echo in yours.'

'Echo in ours?'

'Yes, didn't your god sacrifice himself to himself? On a gallows tree?'

Anwid turned her gaze up to the rafters to think about this for a moment, and it was held by the sight of rows of iron vessels lodged on the narrow beams—rather precariously, she thought. She knew what they were for. Such containers were used to hold boiling pitch, to be poured over marauders. No steam rose from them now. They were surely cold and empty. Still, if they fell on a person's head …

'Are you expecting an invasion?' she asked, pointing upwards.

'Not tonight,' Askr reassured her. 'Not as you have come in peace. But we're ready when *they* come.'

'Who? When who come? No offense intended, but the only invaders we watch out for are Vikings.'

'And we,' Embla said, smiling sweetly, 'watch out for Christians. Not Christians who aren't sure how Christian they are, like you. We mean real Christians.

The people sent by the Pope. The black monks. The missionaries. They are trying to spread Christianity everywhere,'

'When they come, we'll have a reception ready for them that the Pope himself will hear about,' Askr growled threateningly—but at once his fierce expression turned amiable again. 'Let me pour you some more ale, dear lady,' he said. 'And then if you please you will tell us your story—how you came to lose your ship'

After what she had learned about Castle Yggdrasil and its lord and lady, she knew it would not be easy to tell honestly—but still managed to tell it—the story of how the famous Viking Bjarwulf, the Terror of the Seas, had boarded her ship, taken her cargo and all those who sailed in her on to his own ship ('his perfectly splendid ship', she said, 'the Serpent King') and then set fire to hers. She felt it necessary to put in: 'He treated us all with great respect and generosity. He brought us—me and my girls—to a beach not far from my home. I have no complaint against the great Viking or his crew. I understood. It's his living, pirating. It's an honoured profession among Vikings. Living by plunder—I mean, that's what they do. But I only wish he had not set fire to The Good Ship Good. We were not far from England when we abandoned her, so I think we may find her somewhere along the coast.'

'A burnt out wreck?' Askr said, not unsympathetically.

'She's very stout. And if there were high seas, waves could have swamped her and put out the fire. And her timbers are too well-seasoned to catch fire easily. I think she will not be burnt out. Just scorched.'

'What did he take from you?' Askr inquired.

'Well, everything—but we didn't have much. His accountant—who it seems always sails with him—assessed our entire cargo, mostly straw, a little wine, garlic, at less than the price of their whole voyage. But—well, it was the gels, you see. As it turned out. That's what he they valued. The gels.'

'*Those* girls?' Askr and Embla both asked at the same time.

'No, no. Not those gels. Those were the ones they left with me. The other gels. The—the—'

'The flowers of the crop?' Embla suggested.

Anwid looked down and said nothing. She knew what was coming next, and it came. Embla, Askr, all those at the table, and even the servants bearing platters and jugs, laughed aloud.

Anwid raised her voice. 'There was a Viking left on board,' she called out.

The laughter stopped at once.

'One of the pirates?' Embla asked.

'No, one of our passengers. We were carrying two Vikings. We only found out later—too late—when we disembarked in England—that one had been left behind. We dread to think of it, but he may have perished in the fire.'

Noises of consternation were sounded on all sides.

Anwid raised her voice even higher. 'One of the main reasons we need to find the ship is to find him. If he is not to be found on her, we will assume he is alive, and continue our search for him.'

'Of course,' Askr said. 'He must be found.'

'What's his name?' Embla asked.

'Mordec.'

Embla frowned. 'That's not a Viking name. Not that I've ever heard.'

'Mordec—son of Hauk,' Astrid said hastily.

'Now *that's* a Viking name—Hauk,' Embla said. 'We'll help any way we can to find your missing Viking passenger. We'll post look-outs for your ship. We'll patrol our beaches.'

'That would be good!' Anwid said.

Askr refilled her cup, smiling.

Embla said, 'Now for some more entertainment.'

Again she clapped three times.

While they had been talking, a tree had appeared in the middle of the floor. Not a tall tree: a big-boled tree with white roots snaking along the floor, and soft branches holding up bundles of soft green leaves. The whole plant was made of cloth. As music was struck up somewhere out of sight on small drums and shrill flutes, the tree began to shiver, then to wave its branches about—and then to dance. It float-ed over the floor, paused and swayed, floated again, this way and that. The roots jiggled, the branches dipped and rose. Until the music stopped abruptly. The tree stood still. To the sound of cracking wood, made somehow by the invisible band, the bole split open, and two figures were revealed inside it, one male in clothes so molded to his body that at first glance he would seem to be naked, and one female with long yellow hair covering her from crown to foot like a cloak. Both wore black masks with holes to see through. The woman's eyes were as black and shiny as the jet beads that studded Askr's sword and hung in rows on Embla's bosom.

They stepped out of the tree, stripped off the masks, and holding hands they bowed to the lord and lady.

'Askr and Embla!' many voices exclaimed with delight as everyone applauded.

The male was the boy who had sung to them. The female was a young girl.

'Sven and Charlotte,' Askr called, 'come and get your rewards.' They came to the table and Askr put a purse into the outstretched hand of each. They bowed, laughed, and skipped away.

'The boy is the son of the captain of the guard,' Askr told Anwid. 'He looks like a willow branch, but he's one of our best fighters. I've seen him twist the head of a sinewy little priest and drop the corpse to the ground with no more strain than if he had been breaking the neck of a foul.'

'The girl.' Embla said, 'is a wandering entertainer. She told me she has been in France and Italy, and has travelled with Vikings on sea and land, and came to England with a princess, and dances for a living.'

That night, when the hall was empty of all but themselves, Anwid told her girls to say only kind things of Vikings, even of Bjarwulf, while they were in the castle. 'And don't say any prayers—or not so anyone can hear you.'

'None of us ever does,' Dellibeth said. 'Do we?'

'No,' came the reply in a breathy chorus.

'Never have, never will,' one of the others said quietly.

'That's good' Anwid said. 'But the vital thing is—don't start now, or we may not see the morning.'

They did see the morning. And when they were all assembled in the yard, waiting for the portcullis to be raised and the moat lowered, Askr appeared, clad in a long striped garment and a nightcap to match, his feet in leather slippers. He led a line of servants bearing packages wrapped in green leaves tied with yellow ribbons, which they pushed into the girls' bundles.

'Food for the road,' he said. 'Dried fish. Be careful of the bones.'

He turned to Anwid.

'If we should find the Viking … if we should see your ship …'

Anwid delivered her usual plea to her hosts of the night on parting: 'Moor her, I beg you. You can't fail to know her if you see her. She is like no other ship—almost as broad as she is long, and with her rudder in the stern. And on both sides of her bows her name, The Good Ship Good, is spelt out in iron studs that won't have been hurt by fire.'

'But how shall we let you know if …?'

'Pray send a messenger to Felldown. My father will reward him.'

'And your father will …?'

'Get word to me, yes.'

'Then as you say,' Askr promised.

When all the words of farewell and thanks had been said, Anwid led her plain but serviceable girls through the arch, over the net, under the points of the raised portcullis, and out across the bridge, noticing now that the winter sun was shining palely on the water that there were huge fish with sharp teeth patrolling the moat. They might have been sharks.

'Hold it!' a voice shouted, 'don't bring in the bridge, I'm going with them.'

'It's the Dancer!' Dellibeth cried out.

Yes, only a dancer could run so lightly along the bridge which had been withdrawn a short distance from the bank. It was her. It was the girl named Charlotte. Her hair was not yellow and thick and straight now but black and curly. Wrapped up in woollen—though sleeveless—garments, and with a large leather wallet strapped to her back, she ran to the edge and, with a most graceful leap, sailed through the air and landed on the bank, on one leg, beside Anwid, the other leg stretched out behind her, her arms weaving about lithe and white as the necks of swans. Laughing, she brought her feet together and took hold of Anwid's arm with both her hands.

'I like to travel in good company,' she explained. 'I don't feel safe all on my own. And by the way, my eyes are very keen. If there's a ship to be seen, I'll see it. And as for Mordec son of Hauk—I know him well. Me and him, we fought side by side against a fearsome enemy and we won. I'll tell you the story as we go.'

a royal welcome

When the fog below them cleared away, a wide green valley appeared to Mordec and Leif.

'How far down would you say it is?' Mordec asked his clear-eyed companion. 'About as far as we came up?'

'We'll have further to go to reach the bottom,' Leif said, lying prone and hanging his head over a ledge—not because he needed to in order to see to the foot of the mountain, but just to feel what it was like to peer over a ledge that way. 'But the mountain isn't so steep on this side. And not nearly so rocky. There are some quite easy ways down.'

'Let's go,' Mordec said, shouldering his sack which was now quite light.

Leif as usual went in front, to see the way. It did not take him long to find the fun in exploiting the power Mordec had given him.

'This way will be the easiest, this way for sure.'

'Between these stones? The other side seems wider.'

'Oh no! Believe me, Mordec, it's really slippery there. I know this is a bit of a squeeze but it's safer. Really truly … Sure you can—I'll pull you. Well yes, you did get a bit of a scratch on your hand. Sorry … This way. Yes, it's shadowy here but I can see. Just a little further. Almost through. Oh! Hmm—well, I was wrong. There's no way out. It's a cave. We'll have to go back. … Oh! It's *a bit* steep down here. Whoops! Wheeee! That was fun wasn't it, sliding down on our bums? Yes, it was *a bit* sore. Yes, it's torn *a bit*, well *quite a bit*, but it's not *too* bad.'

'I'm beginning to think I'm more likely to reach the bottom in one piece if I feel my way down rather than trust you to guide me,' Mordec said.

When they did reach the bottom the going was easy over grassland, though the grass was tall, at times taller than Leif. But no farmsteads, no cattle were to be seen.

'Horses?' Mordec asked Leif. 'Wild horses maybe?'

'No. No animals at all. Just birds.'

'Strange,' Mordec said. 'Such fertile land.'

Something he could not fail to see were the mountains on the other side of the valley. More mountains! But the range sloped towards the south.

'We'll go that way, 'he decided. 'Slate said there is a port to the south where Viking trading ships put in.'

'He said it's a long way,' Leif reminded him.

'But it will be easier than climbing over the mountains. And with you as a guide I don't think I'd have much hope of surviving the attempt,' was Mordec's reply, which for some reason Leif found funny.

'At least you're a cheerful companion,' Mordec remarked, giving him a pat on the back.

Southward they trudged for two days, by which time all the bread—hard though it had become—and almost all the ham was gone. The boys were filthy, their clothes torn, and after another night, hungry too. But when early on the third morning they got through a thicket between two low hills, they found some comfort and joy.

'A great shining!' Mordec exclaimed. 'You needn't tell me what it is. I know by the smell. I know by the sound. We have come to the sea. We are back on the west coast of Wales.'

Cold as the water was, they bathed. Then, clad again in their grimy clothes—which they did not dare take off and wash because they'd take too long to dry while the boys would be waiting naked and freezing—they took turns gnawing on the last ham bone and scratching up crumbs from the bottom of the sacks.

'What'll we do now, Mordec?'

'We'll wait here for a while. Maybe we'll see a ship. We'll hail it and they'll send a boat to rescue us. Then we can work our passage to any port they're headed too. English port or French port, it doesn't matter which, because from there we're sure to find a ship to take us home.'

'I'm hungry,' Leif said.

'You're always hungry,' Mordec said. 'Greedy, that's what you are. If you hadn't been so greedy we'd have some stuff left.'

'Can we catch fish?' Leif asked.

'No. But we can get shellfish off the rocks.'

They ate the shellfish raw. The slimy things had little effect on Leif, but they made Mordec feel sick.

'Look out for a ship,' he instructed Leif as he lay down and closed his eyes. 'I'm going to lie here on this rock with one sack under my head and the other on top of me and I'm going to groan. If I die, keep watching. A ship will come. You'll survive.'

Leif brought his head down close to Mordec's. 'Don't die, Mordec, please,' he said, trying to prize one of the closed eyelids open with a finger and thumb. 'I'm sorry I led you through those bad places. I didn't mean for you to get hurt.'

'I forgive you,' Mordec said. 'Now let me sleep.'

Leif positioned himself to watch both the sea and the sleeper.

Mordec did not know how long he slept, but the sun was past its zenith when he woke and found Leif still sitting faithfully in the same place.

'Come,' Mordec said. 'We must find fresh water. And food. We'll go inland. There must be a town or something near here.'

Leif laughed in his relief at having Mordec back with him, alive and strong again.

'This way,' Mordec commanded, starting eastward toward some dunes. The boys' feet sank into the sand and their progress was slow. But beyond the dunes they came to a hill, and it was easy to climb. There was grass, and there were small bushes to hold on to, and even some stunted trees with rough bark and thick grey leaves. When the sun began its setting in a blaze that spread across the whole sky, they reached the summit, a line of flat-topped red rocks.

'I hear something,' Mordec said 'I think it's singing. Or is it just the wind in the rocks? It comes and goes on the breeze. No, it's definitely singing. Look over the top and tell me what you see. Carefully, please. We don't want anyone to see us. Not yet. Not until we know if they're friendly.'

Leif climbed until his nose was on a level with the flat top of a rock. 'I see people,' he said. 'I see houses with people standing in front of them, and—yes, they are singing.'

'All of them?'

'In front of every door of every house there is a person—some houses have two or three people—and they're all just standing there singing. And looking at us.'

'At us?'

'Well looking up at where we are. I don't think they can see me looking at them.'

'Men or women?'

'Both.'

'What are the houses like?'

'Not big but nice. White. With different colour-ed doors. And gardens. And some geese. And a pig. And some dogs.'

'Dogs? How big?'

'Small.' Leif showed a length and height with his hands.

'Can you hear what they're singing?'

'No.'

'What about their clothes?'

'What d'you mean?'

'What sort of clothes are they wearing?'

Leif shrugged. 'Just clothes. Some of them are carrying lanterns.'

'Lit? It's not dark yet!'

'No. Not lit.'

'Then I wonder what they need to carry lanterns for. What colour is their hair?'

'Can't see. Most of them are wearing caps. There's a woman with yellow hair and a woman with grey hair who aren't wearing caps.'

'Do the men have weapons? Swords? Clubs?'

'No.'

'Then I think we will be safe. We'll ask them for food and lodging. We'll offer to work for them. You ready?'

'Ready.'

'Then let's stand up and wave and shout—we must try to make them see us.'

'What'll we shout?'

'Hullooo. Many times. Until we know they've seen us. *Now!*'

They rose, stepped up on to the flat stones, raised their arms high, waved them about and shouted, 'Hullooo! Hullooo!'

The singing died away and stopped. So they had been heard.

'What are they doing?' Mordec asked, while continuing to wave.

'They're just standing there looking at us. Now they're moving. They're all moving. They're coming towards us, they're running now, and they've begun to shout.'

'I can hear them shouting. Do they seem angry?' He looked about him. 'Where can we hide?'

'They're not angry. They're waving and smiling. They're glad to see us, I think. More people are coming out of the houses now. They're all running towards us, and they seem happy. Some of them have started climbing. Shall we run away?'

'I don't think we could get very far. Let's try smiling back at them. Stand and smile. And if they grab us, don't fight back. Let them take us prisoner if that's what they want.'

So the two of them stood stiff and still on their rocks, arms at their sides, their teeth bared in fixed grins, braced for assault of some kind.

But what happened was the last thing they could possibly have expected. When the climbers, first four, then six, then more strong stocky young men, reached the flat space in front of the row of rocks, they stopped still, swept off their hats, and bowed low, still smiling. Then they fell on their knees and began clapping their hands. More men, and women and boys and girls came up behind them, and did the same, until the whole hillside was covered by people on their knees, clapping. And in the valley a bell began to peel, and went on and on peeling, as though to proclaim a victory.

Leif laughed and looked at Mordec. Mordec looked back at him in bewilderment.

'Hullo again!' Mordec said, conversationally, to the man kneeling nearest to him.

The man bowed his head, unclasped and reclasped his hands and lifted them towards Mordec as though appealing for something.

'Look.' Leif said. 'Now they're bringing a chair up here. On poles. Two rows of men are carrying it. Can you see it?'

'I see something coming. I see people standing up and making way for the thing.'

The crowd made way for the chair—a grand and gilded thing with cushions and a crown on top of the backrest. When it was put down in front of Mordec, a figure was revealed panting up behind it; a man in a rich black robe and large domed hat, with gold chains hanging round his neck.

He bowed low to Mordec, but did not fall on his knees.

'Your Highness,' he said, 'Welcome! We were expecting you. We have never stopped expecting you. We have never lost hope of your return, not for a day or an hour. If it please Your Highness, will you take your place on the carriage-throne?'

He stepped aside and reached an arm out towards the chair.

Even more bewildered, and thinking that this hospitality went beyond anything he'd ever heard of or imagined, Mordec said, 'Thank you,' and did as he was asked.

'Er …' He pointed to Leif.

'Your page will accompany you, of course, Your Highness.'

'Come on,' Mordec said, beckoning Leif to hurry.

There was plenty of room on the grand chair for Leif to perch on it beside Mordec, which he did. The chair was picked up by the two rows of bearers, and a slow and dignified descent from the hill-top began, with the man in black walking in front of them and two lines of men in armour, with spears on their shoulders—who had seemed to Mordec to have emerged suddenly from nowhere—marched behind.

When the reached the bottom of the hill they started along a road that sloped slightly upwards. Leif leant forward and turned his head from side to side in a state of considerable excitement. Crowds of people stood on either side in front of the houses, waving and cheering as the chair passed between them. All the faces were glowing with happiness. Dogs barked. The sun sank, stars came out, and they moved on in twilight.

Mordec was in a quandary as to whether he should wave back or not. He decided friendliness never did any harm, and he politely waved, first this way and then that, and smiled as amiably as he could—while yet wondering whether he and Leif were being transported to glory or to death. It was, he thought, possible that they treated captives this way before executing them.

Little lights appeared in people's hands, thousands of them flickering and glowing. Some young men ran beside the chair, laughing and whooping. A band of drummers and pipers fell in behind the armed guard and began to play, and all at once the crowd began to sing to the music. It was a happy song this time—though Mordec could make out no words except an oft-repeated 'home'.

Leif could see they were approaching a house much bigger than all the rest, lit up by flaming torches.

'They're taking us to a huge house,' he murmured in Mordec's ear. 'I think it's a palace. Yes, it's a palace, Mordec. And it's got green walls. And there's a yellow flag with a black O on it waving on the roof.'

They passed through iron gates and went on between rows of armed guards. The crowds were left behind at the gates, and so too was the band, though it went on playing, and the people went on singing. On the threshold of a grand entrance whose doors were opened wide, Mordec could see a figure standing against the light of the hall.

'Is it a man or a woman, Leif?'

'A woman,' Leif said with conviction as they came closer and he saw her long hair, her trailing skirts, and a band of glinting gems circling her head.

'A woman. You're sure?' Mordec's feeling of relief was instant and welcome—but unreasonable, he told himself. A woman could be as dangerous as a man, he had cause to know.

He was handed down from the chair by the man in black, who led him up some steps to stand before the woman. She regarded him steadily for a few moments, smiling all the while, then took a step forward and stretched her arms towards him.

'Welcome home, dear brother!' she called; and as she embraced him, she pulled him gently towards her and whispered in his ear, 'I'll explain'. Then she kissed him on each cheek, gripped his arm lightly, turned him towards the open doors and trod ceremoniously with measured steps which he had no choice but to match, into a great hall lit by hundreds of wax candles in silver brackets along the walls.

The man in black followed them, and gestured to Leif to follow him.

The woman did not let go of Mordec's arm, nor alter her gait or pace over the marble floor until they reached a dais where, under a canopy, two thrones stood, each with a carved and gilded crown on the backrest, the one a little smaller than the other. The woman steered Mordec to the larger one, let go of him, and seated herself on the other.

Mordec, understanding perfectly well what was expected of him while failing utterly to imagine why, sat on the crimson cushions, holding himself stiffly as she did.

The man in black stood before them, bowed, and spoke out in ringing tones, so all the guards who had taken up positions along the walls under the candle brackets, and all the finely dressed ladies and gentlemen who had entered through inner doors and now stood about on the marble floor facing them, could hear what he said.

'Your Highness, I am more glad than words can describe to have lived long enough to see this day of your return to us. You seem a little dazed, sir, and who can wonder at it? And you have lost your eyeglasses, which is why you did not greet me or your sister by our names, of course.'

'My eyeglasses?' Mordec said. 'Yes, right, I have lost them! Are there any … any of my eyeglasses here? I mean, could someone fetch a pair for me?'

'Certainly, sir. Of the twelve pairs kept in the royal chamber, all but one—the pair you took with you, sir—are in their place.'

He beckoned to a young boy dressed in scarlet and murmured an instruction to him. The boy hastened away.

'You will soon be able to see that it is I, Cadfan the Chamberlain, your old servant, who stands before you, and that beside you sits indeed your sister, the Princess Angharad.'

'Oh, I will, yes,' Mordec said. 'Er—greetings, Cadfan. I too am glad … to see you again. I was very moved by the reception of the … people. And above all—of course—I'm happy to see you again, dear sister.'

The Princess looked back at him with laughing eyes, and pinched her lips together to stop herself laughing.

But Leif—who was standing behind Cadfan—was capable of no such restraint. On hearing Mordec claiming the Princess's as his sister, he burst out laughing.

Cadfan looked back at him with a frown.

'Control yourself, boy!' Mordec said sternly.

Leif covered his mouth with both his hands.

'I'm sorry to say, Cadfan, that my page has for-gotten his manners. He is laughing because he is as pleased as I am to be … er … home again.'

At this moment the page who had been dispatched to fetch the eyeglasses returned with them on a round crimson cushion trimmed with golden cord and em-broidered with a large golden M on it! What could the M stand for, Mordec wondered. No one had called him by a name.

Cadfan the Chamberlain took the cushion and proffered the eyeglasses to Mordec.

He lifted them with caution, shut his eyes, placed the pair on his nose, then sprang his eyes open. The clarity was almost frightening. The glass made everything look too big, too close. They were not what he would have chosen to help his myopia, but they erred on the right side. At least in terms of size—width between the eyes, length of the shafts—they sat comfortably enough. They would do. They would have to do.

'Now, Madoc, all you need is to put on some proper clothes, and you'll feel like yourself again,' Angharad said. She spoke loudly, though he was right there beside her—obviously to be sure everyone in the hall could hear her. 'Let your pages attend you to your quarters, and later we will celebrate your homecoming.'

An hour later, washed, combed, and dressed in princely garments, Mordec sat at a well-laden table on a gilded chair between Angharad and Cadfan, taking in quantities of what Angharad told him were his favorite foods.

He saw Leif among the servants, also clean and combed, dressed in the scarlet livery of the house, and looking perfectly contented—'Which means he's already swallowed an enormous dinner,' Mordec thought. Catching Leif's eye, he winked before turning away. It was a way of saying, 'We're in this adventure together.' They were two among many strangers; their loyalty was to each other; but, Mordec was signalling, 'Play along with them.'

Dinner over, Angharad led Mordec to a small room lit only by a brisk bright fire burning in the grate. They reclined on couches covered with the furs of foxes, on either side of the high stone hearth. Small dogs, long in the body and short-legged, with smooth white and tawny coats of long hair, lay before the fire or shared her couch.

Her brown eyes shone in the firelight. Her hair was a dark red colour that he had seen only once before, and that on a man: the Red Magician, Sam of the West. She was good to look at, and she had a soothing voice.

'Now,' she said. 'Tell me who you really are.'

'I'm glad you asked,' he replied. 'I'll tell you who I am, and then you must tell me who it is everyone takes me for. Everyone but you, that is.'

'Agreed. What is your name?'

'Mordec son of Hauk. I'm a Viking. The boy with me is a Viking too. We … got lost, and are trying to find our way home.'

'We have all night,' she said 'You can take your time and tell me the whole story.'

'I will. I promise. But I must know—who do they think I am? A lost brother of yours—that much I've gathered. A prince—a beloved prince. But why do they think I'm that person? To tell the truth, I feel rather bad about posing as someone I'm not—even though you more or less told me to do it. I need to know the reason for that—why you want to keep up the … act. The play. The pretence.'

'You may find it hard to believe this, Mordec son of Hauk, but you are now the ruler of this little princedom. You are rich, you are loved by the people, and you have all the burdens of a ruler to bear. All the duties to perform. But don't worry—I and Cadfan will guide you through them.'

'Cadfan? Does he know that I'm … acting the part?'

'Yes. I'll explain why it's necessary for us to keep you here as my brother, the monarch.'

'Keep me here?'

She was silent for some moments, her white long-fingered jewelled hand slowly stroking a dog that had curled up beside her.

Then she said, 'The job of a monarch has its rewards, Mordec. This palace is comfortable. Our servants are loyal. Our people are prosperous and pay their taxes. They are also a happy lot on the whole—though they have been sad for the last ten years. The length of time you've been gone.'

'Ten years? How old do they think I am?'

'They think you are fifteen—the age you were when you went away, taking one of the pages with you. You climbed the hill early one morning and disappeared. The hill opened and took you in. Because even the earth loved you, and wanted you to itself. And inside the hill time stands still. So although my brother was born only four years after me, I am twenty-nine and he is still fifteen.'

'They believe that? All of them?'

'Yes, they believe that. All of them.'

'But—do I look like him?'

'You're a fifteen year old boy. That's resemblance enough after ten years. And you've got poor eyesight. Amazing luck!'

'What do you think happened to him?'

'I think he escaped. Ran away. Found freedom. Where and how I have no idea.'

'*Escaped?*'

He was asking her, in a tone that was puzzled, amused, slightly shocked, to say more. But she let that pass. Her hand went on without pause stroking the dozing dog.

He asked a different question.

'Do you think he is alive?'

'I don't know. But I'm certain he'll never come back.'

'What was his name?'

'Madoc. Near enough—by good luck—to your own name for you to answer when addressed by it unexpectedly.'

'I haven't said that I—

'I've told you what you wanted to know.' She said more briskly as she changed her position. The dog stretched out too. 'Now your story, please.'

'There are still so many things I don't know and really need to.'

'You can ask me any questions you like, in private. I promise to answer them all.'

'One last one for now. What was the page's name?'

'Lefan.'

'Odds-bods! The boy with me is called Leif.'

Angharad laughed. 'Perhaps you really are my brother Madoc, just a little changed by your ten year sleep in the hill.'

'I'll have to tell him the story.'

'Can he keep a secret, d'you think? If the truth gets out that you are not Madoc, that he is not Lefan—if the people were to doubt you, I can't answer for what they might do.'

'To you or to me?'

'To both of us. You'd better make sure Leif understand that his life may depend on his being Lefan from now on.'

'Didn't Lefan have parents? Won't they know he's not …?'

'He was an orphan. That's what we do with orphans. We take them into service here at the palace. Only I and Cadfan will know he's not the same Lefan who went away with Madoc all those years ago.'

'Right. So what you're telling me is—I'll have to stay awhile?'

'You'll have to stay. Yes.'

'I can't stay too long. I have to get back home.'

Angharad rose and went to stand before the fire looking into the flames, saying nothing. When she had snuggled back among her furs, she said, 'Your story now.'

And Mordec told enough of it to explain how he came to be where he now found himself.

a taste of power and honey

Mordec did not mind at all that the bed he woke in was large and downy; that servants brought him goose-legs and sliced apples on silver platters and ale in a crystal chalice; led him to a marble bath full of warm lavender-scented water; shaved him, combed his hair; and clad him in garments made of soft stuffs in rich colours, embroidered with gold thread. Since the part of a prince had been assigned to him, he thought, why not enjoy it?

'The lavender scent is too strong in the steam,' he said, recalling Lord Alger's complaint. 'We'll have jasmine next time.'

He asked for all the eyeglasses to be brought to him, which they were on a large tasseled cushion—nine pairs in all—and he tried them on. In each pair the glass was of a different thickness. None was quite as good as those he had lost, but he found the pair that suited him best and wore them. At once his strength and confidence returned. He realized how insecure he had felt in a world of uncertain shapes.

'I think we'll stay here for a few days,' he said very quietly to Leif when they were alone together. They were waiting for horses to be brought to them by grooms for a ride up the valley, between the sunlit hills, in the middle of the cold bright day. 'Maybe a week or two. After all, there's no hurry for me to get home. I sent a message that I was on my way. My father and mother will have it by now. They won't be worried about me.'

'Why don't we stay for ever?' Leif whispered back. 'It's not bad, is it? I mean—well, tell me—is it as nice as this at home?'

Mordec did not reply. He felt the same temptation as Leif to accept and enjoy their good luck, but became too aware of a nagging little thought in the back of his mind that he was being dishonest with the people here—an uncomfortable fact, even though it made them happy—and, at the same time, somehow disloyal to his own people.

It was from Leif—who had guzzled three lavish meals in the servants' quarters where he'd listened to what was said rather than chatter as he liked so much to do—that Mordec learnt, as they rode side by side with two mounted guards ahead and the two grooms behind, about the nation he now, by strange chance, officially ruled over.

'They say that we were gone so long we've forgotten how to say our names properly,' Leif told Mordec. 'Hee! It's funny, because they're the ones who can't say our names properly. They call me Lef-*an*, and they call you Prince Mad-doc. They think we were born here and were captured by the hill and held prisoner inside it for ten years. They want me to tell them how we escaped.'

'What did you tell them?'

'I didn't tell them anything, honest I didn't, Mordec. I'm not stupid. I mean, if I go and tell them that we aren't who they think we are—well, they won't be too pleased will they? I think they might stop being so nice to us. They might even hack us up into tiny pieces or something. I only told them everything that happened to us inside the hill has been magicked out of our memories.'

'And they believed you?'

'Yes, I know they did because they nodded. They nodded at me like this—and at each other—so I s'pose that's what they …'

'Expected to hear?'

'S'pose so.'

'Did you find out why they were singing?'

Leif knew that too. And Mordec, listening patiently, gradually pieced together a more complete story than Angharad had outlined for him.

Here it is, better told, for all you studious historians:

Prince Madoc was a good prince, a kind and happy prince, with only one fault—he could not see well. But by lucky chance, traders had come to the valley and among their merchandise they had pieces of glass fixed together so a person could wear them in front of his eyes and they would help him to see.

His forefathers had lived in the palace—a green palace with a copper roof that time had turned pale green—at the north end of the valley since time had begun.

One day, when he was fifteen, he left the palace at dawn. He was an early riser and would often go out walking or riding with just a page to keep him company.

'I'll be back before the sun sets,' he'd told the watchmen at the gates. He and the page were seen climbing the western hill and stepping over the stones at the top.

As the sun began to set, the people of the court lined up outside the palace doors ready to welcome him back. 'But the sun set, the stars came out, and he did not return,' in the words of the song that the old court musician, Gwyn Gwilym, composed before he died in sorrow.

Cadfan the Chamberlain sent servants and guards to search for the Prince with lanterns. They searched all night, but he was nowhere to be found.

For days after that the people of the farms and the town would go out in groups, and search as far as they could while daylight lasted, some even coming home late at night 'with lanterns in their hands and sorrow on their faces', as the song related.

The Prince had been gone for only a few days when the custom of singing to him was started by Gwyn Gwilym himself. He stood outside the palace gates, facing the hill, and sang his song. Next day he was joined by a few others; and it wasn't long before everyone learnt the song, even the rich and grand.

It became the custom for folk to sing it together as they came home from work, many of them believing that the more voices there were pleading for the Prince's return, the more likely it was that their wish would come true; that the song itself, when sung in chorus by many voices, had magic *powers, and if they sang it regularly, ritually, for long enough, proving their faithfulness over time, its magic would work and the prince would return. Singing, they trailed down the road to where their small white houses stood in rows.*

They stood at their doors, their faces lifted to the sinking sun, and continued singing, most beautifully, the different registers in perfect harmony, the descants as high and sweet as if they came from a source of music in the sky, until darkness flooded the valley. Then, as the last notes sank away and the final echo faded on the hill, they'd turn one and all into their houses and close their doors. Soon the stars would shine on a deep silence.

The song called the Prince home. The words and even the tune changed more than a little over time as inspiration struck young poets and composers. But the oft-repeated refrain stayed the same:

> *Prince of our hearts*
> *Come home to us,*
> *We long for you so!*
> *Magic spirits of the hill,*
> *Let our darling go!*

* * *

In the afternoon, wearing a light plain crown of beaten gold and a heavy purple cloak trimmed with white fur, Mordec sat in state and heard petitions: for a post at the palace; for a lease on a royal meadow; for a contract to supply bacon to the royal kitchen, and more—seven in all. The faces of the petitioners and the families they brought with them, women and

136

men, old and young, were all full of—not just hope, he thought, but—certainty that their wishes would be fulfilled, that the Prince would not deny them.

Cadfan the Chamberlain, a stern figure of authority in his black robes and chains of office, bent his head (crowned with that black dome of a hat) and murmured advice in Mordec's ear: 'Put off answering him to another day.' 'Say you would if you could but it's just not possible.' 'Allow her half the measure she's asking for.'

Mordec listened to the whispers, but each time turned back to the petitioner, smiled, nodded, and said 'Yes … sure you can … you may … let's try it …'

When all had been heard and were ready to take their happiness home, Cadfan said loudly so everyone in the hall could hear him, '*His Highness is as generous as ever he was.* Cheers for His Highness Prince Madoc.' And the people cheered, and everyone smiled, and some of the young girls blew kisses to Mordec, and they trooped away with shining eyes and love in their hearts. The hall emptied.

Then Mordec looked up at Cadfan, half expecting a quiet rebuke, but Cadfan only winked at him before striding off with an armful of scrolls.

As soon as Mordec found himself alone, he let his smile go, and he sighed. 'Thing is,' he thought, 'there are at least two people in this place who know I am not Prince Madoc. And they want me to pretend that I am. Why?'

That was the question Angharad had avoided answering the night she had 'explained everything' to Mordec.

He had not seen Angharad all day. He had tried to speak to Cadfan alone before the petitions were heard, but the Chamberlain had turned away, mumbling that he had to fetch something he had left behind, adding they would talk later. 'He's avoiding me', Mordec had understood.

Now he rose, took off the crown and cloak, laid them on the cushioned seat of the throne, and went to sit on the edge of the dais, there to brood with his elbows on his knees and his chin on his fists. But not for long.

In another minute, servants and guards were posting about or taking up stiff positions, and he hastily rose and asked a page to find Lefan. 'Send him to me in my bedchamber. Tell him please to come alone.'

The Prince's robing room was almost as big as his bedchamber. There Mordec began to search chests full of garments and to look among the rows of cloaks on hooks along the walls for his own clothes. Chances were they had been washed and mended and brought here to be stored—out of keeping though they were with all this finery.

'Leif,' he said softly (being careful at all times not to be overheard when talking confidentially to his traveling companion), 'do you know where my own clothes are?'

'They burnt them. Yours and mine. They said they belonged to the hill, and the hill might come for them and take you away again. Can't say I care. I like these better. Why d'you want them?'

'Well, sooner or later we're going to have to leave here and I don't want to take any of their things with me—except these eyeglasses. I won't steal more from them than I have to.'

'Why not?'

Mordec laughed. 'Spoken like a true Viking!' he said, and Leif laughed too. And pursued his idea with some excitement.

'If we have to go we should take all we can carry. Horses. And loads of food and things. You can just order them to bring you horses and food and things. They do whatever you tell them. When are we going? Tonight? Not before supper, please?'

'No. Not tonight.'

'Good,' said Leif.

That evening Mordec and Angharad and the important persons of the court were entertained as they dined by ten singers from the town, five men and five women. They brought offerings: a large basketful of winter vegetables, another of apples from their lofts, and garlands of holly and bluebells. Then they sang a new song, a happy song of praise—composed by all of them, they said—celebrating the return of their prince.

'Perhaps I really *ought* to stay,' Mordec thought, as he held up his chalice to toast the singers, and downed the wine that tasted not unlike his father's mead. 'It would be too unkind to leave them. And Leif wants to stay. But I don't know ...'

He let the chalice be filled again with the honey-sweet wine as the singers prepared to give a second performance by both popular and royal request.

'Well, we'll stay awhile,' he decided, and settled back to enjoy the song, which he did almost as much as if he'd earned the praise.

a deadly shot

The days and nights passed so pleasantly that Mordec forgot to count them. There were the horse-rides, games played with balls and bats, entertainments of song and dance, juggling and acrobatics. The food was varied and excellent, the honey-sweet wine seemed to ensure the sweet dreams he had in his soft warm bed.

There were midnight dances to the music of pipes and drums and stringed instruments. Pretty girls taught him the steps of the dances.

And there was a lady, fair haired, pale eyed, pink skinned, rather large, and taller than he by half a head—which not many people in Owaindale were—who claimed him most often for the dances.

'You have forgotten me, Madoc,' she said, the first time they held hands in a dance. 'The hill has wiped me from your memory and your heart. I am Tegwen, and you and I were betrothed by our fathers when we born in the same month of May, 25 years and nine months ago. It is I will bear the heirs to our princedom,' she said. 'It is in May our betrothal will be formally announced, and it is in June we shall marry. We will be twenty-six, you and I.'

'It's true I have forgotten you,' Mordec said as he watched the movements of her rather large feet in order to copy what she did to perform the dance. 'I have forgotten almost everything. Did you know my father? And my mother? Tell me about them.'

'I never knew your mother,' Tegwen said. 'Her name was Bregus. Princess Bregus, and she died when you were born. And your father, Prince Madoc, died in a hunting accident when you were fourteen. He didn't see too well. He ran after a hart and fell into a deep gorge. Then you became our ruler—for about a year. You were always gentle and laughing. You laughed more then than you do now. Everyone loved you. We love your sister too of course, but not as much as you. She helped you with everything, Helped you to be our judge and ruler. She was always beside you. And then suddenly—you disappeared.'

The next time they were together—Mordec at last enjoying himself as he moved through the figures of the dances—he asked her about her own father and mother. 'My father,' she replied, 'is the richest man in Owaindale. He pays the most taxes. He is called Maredudd the Mine. Most of the copper mines belong to us.'

'Ah!' Mordec said, at a loss for anything better to say.

Later, as he lay in bed, the thought came to him that of course the copper must be sold to buyers beyond this valley. Was it sent eastward to England on pack-horses? If so, there must be a well-used trail.

All his attempts to speak privately to Cadfan and Angharad, to find out why they wanted him to pretend to be Prince Madoc, failed. They were always in a hurry, would be happy to talk to him later … because they knew what he wanted to talk to them about, and were avoiding him. But again, why?

One fine chilly morning, Angharad sent word to him that he and she would go out hunting today. His dresser buttoned him into green hunting wear, carefully placed a green hat with a green feather on his head, and the armourer brought him a bow and a quiver of arrows, a sword, a rope and a horn, and hung them about his person.

Angharad met him in the stable yard. She was dressed in a wide leather skirt, a green jacket, and a hat that matched his. A man, taller than most men in Owaindale, whose boots were so well polished that even on that overcast morning they seemed to radiate a light of their own, bore her bow and quiver along with his own.

She nodded in his direction when they were all three mounted on the glossy tawny horses which would carry them to the edge of the woods. 'Chief Huntsman and Fletcher,' Angharad said.

'I remember you well, Your Highness,' he said. 'You would come and watch me putting the feathers into the arrows when you were about eight years old. I taught you how to fix them in their slots and trim them, and you were soon doing it better than I could with your small fingers. You used to call me "Fletch".'

'Then I'll call you Fletch again, if I may,' Mordec said, and the Chief Huntsman and Fletcher looked pleased, and bowed his head.

Although there were guards and attendants riding with them, some ahead and some behind, Fletch stayed close to Mordec and Angharad; too close to allow him to speak to her about the secret things that troubled him.

But his chance came when they were on foot in the woods, stalking a small herd of roe deer. Agharad now had her quiver on her back and her bow hung on her shoulder. Fletch whispered, 'Let's spread out,' and they did. But Angharad seemed unable to keep advancing in a straight line. Soon she was beside Mordec, and to his surprise—and relief—she said, 'I've brought you out here today because I must talk to you.'

'I've been wanting to talk to you alone for days,' Mordec said. 'But you wouldn't let me.'

'I wanted you to get used to living this life. To being a prince and a ruler. I wanted you to get to like it so much that when I came to tell you that you would never be allowed to leave, you wouldn't mind at all. You'd be glad.'

At that moment a deer leapt over a fallen tree some yards from where they stood. It held its forelegs folded as it rose, and in mid air stretched them out, at the same time folding its hind legs, so it seemed to pause at the top of its rise, and to descend more slowly than it had risen. It landed on its forefeet, and an instant later was on all fours, strolling languidly towards a holly tree. As the deer stretched its neck to browse,

Angharad reached back and seized an arrow, fixed its notch to her bowstring, and sent the missile straight into the deer's neck. It fell without a sound.

'How's that for a killing shot?' she said.

'Deadly,' Mordec said. 'For the deer and me, both.'

Fletch had seen the deer fall, and was hurrying over to it.

'Well aimed, m'lady,' he called, He lifted the dead beast on to his shoulders.

'Take it back to the horses,' Angharad called. 'We'll wait here.'

'Angharad,' Mordec said. 'I like this life. Of course I do. Who wouldn't? It would be very pleasant to go on like this for as long as I live—pretending to be someone I'm not.'

'But? You are going to say you won't do it?'

'I won't do it.'

'You'll deprive these good people of their beloved prince yet again?'

'Is that why you're doing this?' Mordec asked in a tone of disbelief. 'Just to keep your people happy? That's your only reason?'

'Isn't it a good reason? We lost our ruler. We were sad for ten years. Then luck—amazing luck—brought you to us. The people believe you are the same boy who was taken away and then miraculously restored to them. Everything fitted. Your age, your page. Only your speech seemed a little different. But it was you, it was the prince with the weak eyes, it was joy come again. I thought they'd forget. But that song was composed and it became a habit to sing it. It kept their hopes alive. Now they are happy. I cannot let you throw them back again into sorrow and inconsolable distress. You must stay.'

'I cannot,' Mordec said firmly. 'I am truly sorry if I make them unhappy again, but I cannot stay.'

'What do you want that you haven't got? Tell me what it is and I'll see you get it,' the Princess pleaded.

'What I want,' Mordec said, 'is my own life back.'

She shook her head. 'That's the one thing you cannot have.'

'But you can't keep me here,' Mordec said. 'If you tie me up, the people won't be too happy about it—will they?'

'You won't be tied up, But you will not be allowed to leave. There will always be eyes watching you. Every way out of the country will be guarded to keep you in.'

'What if I told the people the truth?'

'You think they would believe you? They *know* that the magic of the hill gave you all sorts of dreams of strange adventures. Try telling them that you raided England, went to save a queen from captivity in Italy and won a battle against overwhelming odds on the way, that you were abandoned on a burning ship by pirates, that you woke on the shore of Wales, that you were smuggled out of Runnydale and came to the top of our hill at exactly that moment of the day by pure chance. Do you think you will convince them? They'll love the stories, but they *know* the truth. Now let's hunt together—and say no more about leaving us. Don't even think of it.'

the twin islands

When the Serpent King had passed the south-east-ernmost point of England, south of the estuary of the River Temese and close to the coast of France, Captain Bjarwulf reckoned—paying more attention to his wishful thinking than to his seadog's instinct—that The Good Ship Good might have drifted westward rather than due south. He was perfectly aware that if she had floated so far as to enter Iberian waters, a strong current would most likely catch her and carry her far out on the vast Sea of Atlantis, and it would be a hopeless task to try and follow here there. He told himself there was at least a fair chance that she was still not far off the coast of England, and might well have been wind-driven as far Cornwall, or even on towards Wales. And besides, Pelf warned him that their supplies were running low and they would need to put into harbour soon to replenish them.

Bjarwulf announced that he was navigating to a spot he knew on the Cornish coast as he believed there was a high chance that was where their quarry had been borne towards, while crew and passengers stood under a fine drizzle on a grey morning.

No one was displeased by the prospect of going ashore, except Hauk, who had some misgivings about the wisdom of daring the Cornish coast.

'What of the Cornish custom of setting false lights to lure ships on to their rocks to wreck them and then plunder them? Are you easy that will not befall us?' he asked the captain respectfully. He had put himself and his quest in the pirate's hands, and needed to trust him; but he knew that many a Viking ship had come to grief on the rocks of Cornwall.

'We'll sail landwards in daylight,' Bjarwulf explained. 'And what I've noticed is, when my ship is spotted from the shore, folk run the other way. I'll not set foot ashore to scare the nation. Pelf and Delfinola will seek supplies, and you will enter the taverns and ask if there have been sightings of The Good Ship Good, or wreckage of her found.'

'Or if they have seen or heard of a lost Viking boy,' Hauk said.

Bjarwulf was an excellent navigator and steersman. He sailed the Serpent King through the afternoon shadow of an island—all of which, except for a narrow beach, was a mountain topped with a castle—into the shallow waters of a bay, where he anchored.

Boats for hire plied between the ships and the shore, picking up sailors and goods. Most of the crew of the Serpent King, and Hauk, Hakon and Gus paid small copper coins to be ferried to the landing-stage, then made for the taverns of the town. Pelf took another ferry-boat when he'd talked the boatman into letting him bring his wife at half-fare, on the grounds that she weighed only half as much as a man. On landing, the two of them went arm-in-arm in search of chandlers with whom Pelf would bargain for a large quantity of smoked meat and biscuit.

The name of the town was Marhasyow. Its people were used to Vikings, whose trading ships often anchored in the bay, though more often in the summer than in these dank days. But Bjarwulf stayed on board with Lars and a few other men to guard the ship. Bjarwulf knew he was not welcome in this town or any town outside his homeland.

Hauk entered the first open door he came to, and joined a row of men leaning on the low wooden wall that separated the stores of flagons and barrels from the thirsty customers.

He listened for a while to their talk. He gathered that they were tin-miners and fishermen and traders. He greeted the fishermen who were nearest to him. They returned his 'Good day!' politely enough, but they looked at him warily. Hauk guessed their thoughts.

He opened his purse, took out silver coins and laid them down, one by one, side by side, along the top of the wooden wall. The host of the tavern heard the sound and came quickly to the customer.

'Give these good men more of what they like,' Hauk said, pointing to the money. 'And a bumper of ale for me.'

They raised their refilled cups to him before they drank, and he decided to come straight to the point.

'You saw the ship that anchored in the bay and you are wondering if I am one of Bjarwulf's men? No. I am a meadmaker. A tavern-owner. We are not on a voyage of piracy. I am in search of my son who was abandoned by mistake on a deserted ship and Bjarwulf has given me passage. Have you seen my son? Has a Viking boy, fifteen years old, been seen, do you know, in these parts?'

They talked awhile quietly among themselves, but returned their attention to him with shakes of their heads.

Hauk placed more coins along the barrier and their tin cups were filled again.

Had they, he asked them, seen or heard of an abandoned ship, almost as broad as it was long, drifting on the tide—or wrecked?

Again they consulted in a huddle, came back and shook their heads.

'There are such ships about. Round ships we call them. But we have seen none abandoned or wrecked.'

'You could ask the King's men,' an old man said. 'They get news from all over the world.'

'The King's men? Are they here?'

'The King is here. In his castle on the island. But you cannot go there now. You must wait for the tide to go out, then you can walk to it.'

'I can walk to the island when the tide goes out?'

'Yes. Then it is no island. You can walk on sand from here to there and your shoes will be dry.'

A memory stirred in Hauk's ale-warmed brain, of a letter Mordec had shown him—the letter that had summoned him on the quest from which he had not returned. It had come from the young English queen named Lily, and there had been something in it about the King of Cornwall.

Recall, recall, Hauk ordered himself.

A wedding. That was it. The King of Cornwall's wedding. And he was no sooner wedded than his bride had vanished. And the King's castle—yes, she had described it, *standing on a rock at the end of a causeway jutting out towards France, and twice every day the causeway becomes swamped by the tide and the rock becomes an island.* Yes, and she also wrote of another castle on another rock off the opposite coast of France. That was where the letter was written for her. Her words had been taken down by the famous magician Sam of the West. No, not by him—by his grandmother. And there Lily was waiting for Mordec. He was to go with her on a journey to no-one knew where, to find her captured mother, the real Queen of the Fenreach. A hopeless undertaking!

'Whyever did I let him go?' Hauk asked him-self—as he had many times since the day Mordec had set out, and every day since he had heard that Mordec was lost.

Sam of the West! Of course Lily would seek his help. He was held in awe by all the world for his knowledge of all things. People sought him out to help them with every kind of quest as if he could know by magic where something—or some-one—lost could be found. It was said that he knew the currents and tides better than most mariners did;

how they flowed, where they flowed, according to the season of the year.

In sudden excitement, roused by hope and ale, Hauk clutched the shoulder of the old man and exclaimed, 'Ah, it is not the King of Cornwall that I need to see, it is Sam of the West, and he is on an island a short voyage east from here!'

The old man stared at the Viking's wide eyes, shook off the hand that gripped him and said, 'You need to get back on board that ship and sleep it off, you crazy Northman!'

'Back on the ship, yes,' Hauk said. He nodded a farewell to the old man, raised an arm in farewell to the others he had been drinking with, and charged out of the tavern and down to the shore. He paid a silver coin to a ferryman to take him at once to the Serpent King without waiting to fill up his boat with more passengers.

the quiet talk that was too loud

Hauk found Bjarwulf rolled top to toe in a bearskin, asleep on his back, his face covered by a light white cloth embroidered with an ornate B. It had been sewn by Delfinola and presented to him before the voyage began. Bjarwulf had accepted it with a laugh. 'What'll I do with this?' he had asked. 'You'll be finding uses for it, I shouldn't wonder,' Delfinola had crooned soothingly.

Its centre pumped up and down as Bjarwulf snored under it. His dome of a belly rose and fell in the same rhythm. By chance, it was the rhythm of the boat's rise and fall on the gently heaving water of the bay, which also rolled an empty flagon to and fro on the boards beside the sleeping pirate.

Lars jokingly put a finger to his lips when Hauk caught his eye.

But Hauk was there to rouse the Captain to action. He knelt beside the sleeping man and rudely shattered the peaceful scene with a bellow close to the ear of the sleeping pirate.

'BJARWULF!'

Bjarwulf woke with a snort and half rose, the bewilderment in his eyes quickly replaced with a look of hate and cunning as his hand fell on the haft of the axe he kept in his belt.

'Hah? What's that? Who?'

Seeing who it was who knelt beside him, he lay back again and replaced the cloth on his face. 'Something happened?' he muttered. 'Something wrong?'

'Bjarwulf, listen. I've just remembered. A few hour's sailing that way—' Hauk lifted the cloth from Bjarwulf's face and pointed east, 'there's a man who can help us find Mordec. His name is Sam of the West. You've heard of him, the Red Magician?'

Bjarwulf sat up again, opened and shut his mouth a few times, reached for the flagon, held it up to the light of the lantern, and seeing it was empty flung it overboard.

'Lars!' he shouted.

Lars—it was he sitting against the main-mast—came promptly at the Captain's call. He loved and admired his master above all men, and aspired to become like him; though he was thin and his master stout; though his hair was scant and fair and his master's was thick and black. But he shaved his head as his master did, leaving a tuft of hair on the crown as his master did. And he was as burnt by the sun as his master, and he stained his teeth red like his master's. He believed that by obeying the great man, and following him in all the ways he could, he too would one day become a famous pirate with his own ship.

'Captain?'

'Water!'

Lars hurried to dip a ladle into a water barrel and carry it to the parched Captain, now sitting and mopping his face with the delicate cloth.

'Send Lars to round up the others.' Hauk urged. 'We must go at once. We could be there by morning. Easy. He lives in a castle on an island—like this one. He will tell us which way The Good Ship Good must have been carried. He will know if Mordec has been seen.'

'I *know*,' Bjarwulf said, 'where he lives. And I also know that in that very same castle on that very same island lives the Abbot Alonso de Llama and his Black Monks. A terrible man. Vicious. He calls me the curse of the seas. He wants to nail me to my own mast and set my ship on fire and float me to what he calls—not Valhalla, no, not where I will surely go to join the heroes, but "Hell", where he says I will burn for all eternity. He has proclaimed it. He sent the word that he's after me round France and Italy and Spain. He said that anyone who brings me alive to him will get a reward of ten gold pieces. He has had my head drawn in charcoal and chicken's blood and pinned up on the walls of taverns.'

'But does he have fighting men at his command?'

'There's a great army of Christians called the Army of the Redeemed that the Pope wants to send to England to make everyone become Christian. And they're building a fleet to take monks and soldiers there. Some of the ships have been lying since last summer in the ports of France. I'll not take my ship within sight of his look-outs. Anyway, this is not the time for a fight. This is a voyage without fighting—as I promised you. I'll fight him when the time is right. It will come soon, the happy day or night when I'll open him up and spread his wings of bone and fix *him* high on *my* mast.'

'Then I must find another ship to take me,' Hauk said.

'There are ships that ply between the two islands. We'll wait for you here. Be sure you're not followed when you return. Dress like a merchant and carry a bundle that could be merchandise for sale.

And that is what Hauk did. Pelf wrapped and corded a merchant's bundle of cloths and bonnets, hose and shawls that Hauk bought at the market in the town.

The night before he left, Hauk asked Gus, for the first time, to tell him something about his travels with Mordec. He drew the boy away from the others. They sat facing each other on the deck, wrapped in furs, a lantern between them.

'You know I am going to ask Sam of the West for help and advice? You and Mordec were on Sam's island. I want you to describe it to me—the castle and the abbey, and what sort of man Sam is. Are they right who say he is full of knowledge?'

It was a very good idea to seek Sam's help, Gus told Hauk several times. Very good. He assured Hauk of the friendliness of Sam and his grandmother, warned him of the malevolence of the Abbot, and described the castle and the abbey in detail.

'You remember it well,' Hauk said.

'We were there twice,' Gus explained. 'Once on the way to Italy—when they hadn't finished building the abbey—and again on the way back.'

'Will you come with me?' Hauk asked.

'The monks might see me,' Gus said. 'They would seize me and try to get me to tell them where Mordec is. Not that I could,' he said ruefully.

'Why would they want to know where Mordec is?'

Gus opened his mouth to answer, but paused. 'To tell you that, I would have to tell you what happened there.'

Hauk was silent as he pondered whether to hear part of Mordec's story from Gus. But what Gus had said about the monks wanting to know where Mordec was—the sense of menace the words conveyed—compelled him to ask for the story.

'Go on,' he said. 'Tell me. What happened? What did Mordec do?'

Too late Gus saw that he had said too much. What he had to say could only make his guilt worse in the eyes of Hauk, only intensify his anger and his grief.

But he could not refuse. So he related how Mordec had dropped a hammer on a monk who was about to kill him, Gus, with an axe.

'So,' Hauk said, 'the Abbott wants Mordec for the murder of one of his monks?'

Gus hung his head and nodded.

'And by murdering the monk he saved your life?'

Gus hung his head lower. 'Yes,' he said. If he was about to receive a blow, he thought, he would not lift a hand to defend himself. When none came, he looked up at Hauk and said, 'It makes what I did later to Mordec even more wicked.'

'Mordec saved your life,' Hauk repeated. 'That makes me very proud.'

Gus looked into Hauk's eyes as best he could by the light of the lantern. He saw the pride there, and no anger. 'Why, yes,' he said. 'It was a great thing that he did.'

'He will be honoured for it,' Hauk said.

'When you tell Sam and his grandmother Djil what I did after we sailed away from the island, to explain why we are searching for Mordec …' Gus began.

Hauk interrupted him. 'Yes, I will have to tell them of course, to explain why we're looking for him.'

'When you tell them, will you say that … that I am ashamed …?' He stopped, gulped, and again hung his head.

Hauk made no reply, but rose and went away. He needed some sleep. The ship he was to sail on was due to leave at dawn on the morrow.

A rowing boat took Hauk and his corded bale from the port where he landed to Sam's island. Hauk stepped ashore on to a small quay, and with his burden of 'merchandise' on his back, started up the path and the steps. Keep left,' Gus had cautioned him, 'right leads to the abbey.'

He passed through open gates and reached a door with a bell hung beside it. He pulled the bell-rope, and after a minute or two the door was opened by a man dressed in red, whom Hauk took to be Sam himself.

'I am Hauk, the father of Mordec the Viking,' he whispered. ('Do not speak loudly,' Gus had said. 'The Abbot has a thousand ears.') Then aloud he announced, 'I bear the cloths and clothes ordered by the Lady Djil from London.'

'Come in,' said Sam (for Sam it was).

Sam and Djil were as friendly as Gus had promised. He explained what he needed to know, and why. He could tell that that they really were as concerned for the fate of Mordec as they said they were. They made no comment on Gus's treachery. Hauk related the event simply, without emotion. He got the impression that Sam was paying attention to every word he said, and would remember it all.

In a high room that commanded a view of the sea and land, Sam unrolled his charts for Hauk to see how currents and prevailing winds moved round England and Cornwall, and how they came round the known world or flowed away from it in and over the vast ocean of Atlantis.

They spoke at all times quietly.

'The walls of this castle are thick, but my neighbour the Abbott has put listening tubes through them,' Sam had warned Hauk. 'They can't hear us if we speak quietly like this.'

'Couldn't you block the tubes?' Hauk asked.

'I could, I know where they are. But I decided to make use of them instead.'

'You mean you …?'.

'Yes. *I listen to them.*'

They both laughed—loudly. 'Let the Abbott wonder what the joke is,' was the thought that crossed both their minds.

But what they did not know was that one word had been heard clearly enough by a listener the other side of the wall between the castle and the Abbey. He had caught the name 'Mordec', and hurried to tell the Abbot.

When Sam and Hauk—with a scroll under his arm—went down to the great chamber where they had dined, Hauk was in a cheerful mood, but anxious to hurry back to Bjarwulf's ship. Sam had told him that for this reason and that reason, because of this chance and that likelihood, The Good Ship Good had almost certainly been carried round Land's End, the promontory of Cornwall which, with the Isles of the Longships not far beyond it, and further away the islands of Scilly, were all that remained of the lost land of Lyonesse. From there it would have been carried slowly up the coast of Wales, Sam concluded, likely as far as the small independency of Runnydale.

'That ship would not have been consumed by fire,' Sam said.

'Especially not at that time of year in those waters. There would have been heavy rain and high seas, waves washing over the deck, putting out the flames. Mordec would have waited for the vessel to come close enough to land before he would attempt going ashore. The coast of Runnydale has long beaches, clusters of rocks, a small fishing-boat harbour—and the people are known to be law-abiding and civil. Seek Mordec there. That is the best advice I can give you.'

'He is alive then? Safe and well?'

'There is no reason to suppose he is not,' Sam replied.

'You have made me feeler happier than I have felt for weeks—ever since I learnt that he was lost.'

'If The Good Ship Good had been shipwrecked, I would have heard of it,' Sam said. 'If burnt remains of her had been seen anywhere, I would have heard of that too. She may yet turn up and sail again under her captain with the crew of girls. But after touching on the coast of Wales, she could have been carried past Ireland and out on to the ocean, in which case she will be lost. But the lone sailor on her—he will have saved himself. He will be found.'

Hauk had never believed in magic powers, and he was aware that Sam could not be sure of what he said; yet he found himself trusting those words—' He will be found'—spoken confidently by a man of Sam's reputation, Sam's obvious authority. He felt as if a heavy burden had been lifted from him. All he had to do now was carry out Sam's advice, follow the route shown to him, and all would be well. He would find his son. They would return to Estrid and Eyrin together.

The men found Djil dressed in a white robe and embroidered shawl from Hauk's opened bale. 'These are gifts for you, illustrious lady,' Hauk had said.

Sam and Hauk complimented her on how well they suited her.

'I make tapestries that tell stories,' she said. 'But I will not weave the story you have told us. Not until I know one day that it has a happy ending.'

Sam and Djil parted from Hauk at their front door, and wished him luck.

They did not wait to wave farewell as the rower began to ply the oars, because someone may have been watching, and would not expect them to wave to a peddler.

Later, when Sam was to learn—listening through the wall between his tower and the Abbey—that secret agents had been sent by the Abbott to follow his visitor, he would rebuke himself, and wonder what mistake he or his visitor had made that had alerted the Abbott to a connection between the 'delivery man from London' and Mordec.

the pampered prisoner

'This must be the strangest captivity that ever was,' Mordec ruminated as he lazed in his warm bath, scented now with jasmine. 'And I must be the most pampered prisoner that ever was.'

His body-servants dressed him in white and put rings of gold and precious stones on his fingers. The new pair of shoes they put on him as they knelt before him, had tiny bells about the ankles. He suspected they were not only for adornment: a dedicated listener could trace his movements by their sound.

He sent the servants and pages away, all but Leif.

They sat side by side on the wide rim of the marble bath.

'You did as I asked?' Mordec said softly.

'It's hopeless,' Leif murmured. 'There are guards posted every few steps along the foot of the hill. New ones came at sunset and they stay all night.'

'Did they see you?'

'I'm sure they didn't, Mordec. I was very quiet. On the way I found a dead rabbit so I carried it in case they found me and asked me what I was doing there. I'd have said I was just rabbit-hunting, you see? You must admit that was clever of me. Don't you think? They didn't see me, but they would've seen me if I'd tried to climb the hill. Anyway, I gave the rabbit to one of the cooks and he cut off one of the feet and told me to keep it for good luck. Look, here it is.' He hauled it from a pocket. 'He said rabbit's feet are sure to bring good luck. He said he's had one all his life and look how lucky he is. I don't think he looks lucky. I wouldn't want to be a cook. But maybe the rabbit's foot helps you get what you want …' His voice was rising as he got carried away by his story.

'Shhh!' Mordec said. 'It's bad about the guards. They're there because she knows I'd try to get away over the hill to the seashore. Every way out will be guarded. She'll have thought of everything.'

Leif did not need to ask who 'she' was.

'So now what will we do? I still think we should just stay.'

'I'll think of another way,' Mordec said. The little bells tinkled. He sat down again. 'I mean to get home. Get back to my own life. But you don't have to come with me. You can stay if you want to. All I ask is that you keep my secrets and help me. You must swear to me you won't give me away. Swear it as a Viking to a Viking.'

Leif got down, stood in front of Mordec and said in a fierce whisper, 'You wouldn't leave me behind! Don't do that! I won't stay here without you. You must remember that you belong to me. Zarath gave you to me. Please, Mordec. You mustn't go without me. Swear it as a Viking to a Viking.'

Mordec laughed.

'As I said, I'll think of a way.'

'For both of us.'

'For both of us. Now, with your permission, *my owner*, I'm going down to dinner. Meet me here again later.'

'*Love* the shoes!' exclaimed one of the younger men of the court, Cledwyn by name, as soon as Mordec entered the hall. Cledwyn was a little taller than most of his fellow grandees, but shorter than Mordec. He considered himself a personal friend of the Prince, though everyone knew he was also jealous of him because—it was assumed—they were rivals for the hand of Tegwen.

'You love these shoes? Oh, then yours they are!' Mordec instantly and warmly responded. 'No, no, I insist. You like them, you have them. No sacrifice at all. Not in the least. We'll swap. I'll have those yellow ones with the upturned toes that you're wearing, and you'll have these with the bells. Our feet must be much the same size.'

Before he had finished speaking he had the white shoes off and was holding them out to Cledwyn, who reached for them laughing at this merry prank of the always generous Prince.

Just then Angharad appeared. She stopped, opened her mouth as if to say something but thought better of it and swept on, elegant in a deep blue gown, Tiny gems glinted in her hair which was dark as night.

She looks like a monarch, Mordec thought. She *is* the monarch. She's ruling this princedom. I'm not. I'm not needed here. What can be the real reason she's keeping me here against my will?

They were locked in quiet battle, he and the princess. All the power seemed to be on her side. But—he vowed to himself—he would win. *There was a way for him to leave. He had just that moment thought of it.*

'Are we to have a dance after dinner?' he enquired of anyone near him who might know the answer.

'No one told me so,' Cledwyn said, 'But why not?' And he went to speak to whomever was in charge of the entertainment.

'Will the usual ladies come?' Mordec asked him when he returned and announced that a dance there would be.

'You mean Tegwen?' Cladwyn said. 'If she does not, I'll fetch her.' But he looked a little dejected as he said it.

It was indeed Tegwen that Mordec wanted to see. Though not in order to woo her, as Cledwyn imagined. Mordec had a more urgent plan in mind.

'I am curious to see a copper mine,' he told her as they paced and turned to the soft strains of a harp. 'I want to go down into one and see what the miners do. Would your father let me do that?'

'I think he'd want to take you down himself and explain everything they do down there. I'll ask him,' she said, 'I'm sure he'd be honoured. What is that tinkling sound? Can you hear it?'

'No.' Mordec lied. 'I can't hear a tinkling sound. I can't imagine what it might be.'

'It's Cledwyn—there—dancing with that clumsy girl Nesta. He's wearing ridiculous shoes. Look—*they're* what's making that noise. Now why does he want to make a fool of himself like that? He really annoys me!'

'Don't let that worry you,' Mordec said. 'About the visit to the mine—I'd like to do it tomorrow morning.'

'I'll have to have at least one dance with him,' Tegwen said coyly.

'While he's wearing those shoes?' Mordec said, at which they both laughed.

a deal is struck

Maredudd, the richest man in Owaindale, bowed very low to Mordec.

He was as dark as his daughter was fair, with his brown skin, black hair, and black eyes; a short man even among short men. But he looked strong. His shoulders were broad, his neck thick, his bare arms brawny. He was dressed like his miners in a single leather garment that fell loosely from his throat to the top of his boots. But unlike his miners—some of whom were gathered behind him—he wore gold rings on his fingers and in his ears.

'Will Your Highness wear this?' Maredudd asked, holding out the uniform leather garment. 'It is very hot and grimy in the mine. Those clothes would be spoilt … yes, cover them … And now if you would please follow me …'

Mordec followed him down a slope and along low passages lit by lanterns hung on hooks in the rock-face, down more slopes and along more passages. Some were so low that even Maredudd had to stoop, and Mordec got down on his hands and knees.

'Our first tunnels were dug by children,' Maredudd said. 'But now we make them so we can stand up-right—most of the way. The copper ore is hauled straight up in buckets through holes. But the men have to come this way with their tools.'

They came to where men were working, hammering chunks of copper ore out of the walls. Others pounded the fallen chunks into smaller pieces. The noise was deafening. Maredudd pointed silently to dark red patches in the grey rock. He put one of the broken pieces into Mordec's hands.

When they came back to the air, they were both wet with sweat. Maredudd led the way to a shed where barrels of water stood ready for the miners to wash themselves, and leather overalls were stacked on shelves. While they washed and put on their clothes, Maredudd told Mordec how the ore was separated from the worthless rock. 'But we don't do much of that ourselves. Nor the smelting. We use very little of our own copper,' he said. 'We sell almost all of it.'

'You send it all over the country? To England? I—I'm sure I knew all this once, but most of my memories are lost.'

'To England and everywhere, Your Highness.'

'But—how?'

'In ships, Your Highness. In ships.'

'Ships? From what port?'

'Sveinsey, where the Vikings come to trade.'

'Ah—ah! Yes. I've heard of Sveinsey. But—how do you get the ore to Sveinsey?'

'Loaded in carts and on mules. Once a week our mule train sets out. It comes back with wine and spices and cloths.'

'Once a week. On which day would that be?'

'Tomorrow. It starts before dawn.'

And so it came about that, very early the next morning, Mordec and Leif, wearing the leather overalls of miners over warm clothes, and miners' boots, and with sacks over their heads which Leif had pilfered from the kitchen stores, brought up the rear of the mule and cart train bound for Sveinsey with a cargo of copper ore. Even with his glasses on, concealed under the sack that covered his head, Mordec found it hard to see in the dim light of daybreak. But he kept close to Leif, following the pumping rump of the last mule.

They were half-way down the main road of the town when a servant in the livery of the palace stepped in front of them and said, 'Pardon me, Your Highness, but Her Highness the Princess Angharad sent you this. She says it is a matter of life and death.'

'Why do you call me "Your Highness"?' Mordec asked, in a deep rough voice.

'The Lord Cadfan said you would be at the back of the mule and cart train with Lefan at your side.'

'He did, did he?' Mordec said in his own voice. 'Well, hand it over then.'

He took off his glasses to read the message, but in the first pale light of dawn he could not see it well enough. He gave it to Leif. 'Read it to me.'

Leif read, slowly, aloud: 'My dear brother, I must see you, Please come. You will not be sorry, I promise. Your loving sister A.'

'Are you alone?' Mordec asked the servant. 'Or are there guards waiting just out of sight with orders to carry me to the palace on a shield?'

'I came alone, Your Highness. My orders are to return with you and Lefan and take you at once to the office of the Lord Cadfan. Her Highness is waiting there.'

Mordec and Leif looked at each other. Whatever Mordec told him to do—go back to the palace, leap on the messenger and knock him down, run and hide—Leif would do. He knew it and he knew Mordec knew it.

Mordec was silent for a long moment. Then he said. 'Let's go to Her Highness.' And he started towards the palace with Leif and the servant close behind him.

When Mordec entered the grand room in which Cadfan spent his working days with vellum and ink, scrolls and books, seals and sealing-wax, the Chamberlain was at his enormous desk, his back to the hearth where a merry fire blazed; and Angharad was seated on one side of the fire. She smiled at Mordec and gestured to the chair opposite her own.

'So it's to be a cosy fireside chat,' he said to himself as he crossed the room and sank into the cushions. 'She has promised I'll be pleased. Let's see.'

'Mordec son of Hauk,' she began, formally but not coldly. 'I understand that it is really not possible for us to keep you here. You know you always have the recourse of telling the people the truth, that you are not their Prince Madoc. It would break their hearts, but it would set you free. I thank you for not having done that. And I must let you go. Before we part, I have a favor to ask of you.'

'I'm listening,' Mordec said.

'I'm asking you to tell one more … little lie, to the people of Owaindale.'

He made no immediate answer. She wanted to search his eyes to gauge his reaction, but the glasses in front of them reflected the firelight and she could tell nothing about his feelings.

'If it does no harm, and if it lets me go, I will consider it,' he said at last. 'So what is it?'

'I want you to make a public address in which you'll say that you, *Prince Madoc*, have decided to go on a journey to complete your education. You will visit many lands, some of them far away. You will be gone for quite a long time. And while you are away, your sister will rule in your stead. She is to be acknowledged by all the people of the realm to be the lawful sovereign and sole ruler, endowed with all the rights, duties, possessions and power of the lawful sovereign. Cadfan is writing out the speech for you to read from the steps of the palace.'

'That's all? And then I can go?'

'Yes. I promise you. You may take horses to bear you and your page, and clothes and provender and arms—and gold and silver and many precious gifts. An escort of mounted guards will be waiting for you at the end of the main road south, and will accompany you until nightfall, so the people can see that you are royally protected. After that—you will have maps to guide you to the port of Sveinsey, where you will find Vikings to greet you and Viking ships to carry you home.'

Mordec took off his glasses and polished them by rubbing them on his leather-covered knee. Angharad did not stir. Cadfan turned his chair and sat looking steadily at Mordec, who had the feeling that both of them were holding their breath.

'Of course I'll do it,' he said.

Angharad took a deep breath and let it out on a sigh of relief.

'But I'm puzzled,' Mordec said. 'Why has it taken you all this time to think of this plan?'

Angharad rose from her chair and went to stand at the high window overlooking the valley and the town. She replied without turning round. There was a touch of sadness in her voice.

'I thought if I could make you really happy here that you would want to stay. Because—well, you see, I really do want to make the people happy by giving them back their prince.'

Mordec thought, 'I have not been fair to her. I thought she was hard and selfish, but I was wrong.'

He went and stood beside her and he too gazed down on the white houses and the tidy gardens, where even he could see patches of the yellow and blue of spring flowers.

'Thank you,' he said. 'I have been happy here. It's a lovely happy country. You have made it so. And you will keep it so.' He turned towards her, smiling. 'I leave it in the best of hands—yours, dear sister of a brief time—far steadier and stronger and kinder than mine will ever be.'

She faced him, meeting his smile with her own, but also with tears in her eyes.

'There was a moment—when you said you needed the eyeglasses—when I thought it really might be possible that you were my brother Madoc come back to me. But of course I knew it wasn't so, and the more I saw of you, the sorrier I became that my scheme was impossible and I must let you go. May you have a good journey, Mordec son of Hauk,' she said, 'and a long life.'

They embraced. And when Mordec turned to leave the room, he saw Cadfan, that proud stiff dignitary, wiping a tear from his own cheek with the tip of an inky finger.

At noon that day, mothers and children and elderly citizens, and those working men who could take a short rest from their labors, gathered in the wide space before the palace, in obedience to a royal summons which heralds had proclaimed through the town.

Many yellow flags with a large black O on them were raised on tall poles inside and outside the gates, waving gaily under a clear blue sky in a brisk breeze.

The crowd cheered when, to the sound of horns, their Prince—handsomely dressed in dark blue tunic, leggings, and fur-lined cloak, his boots polished to such a glow they could have been made of glass, and with a sword at his side—stepped out holding the hand of the Princess. She wore a blue gown, and a circlet of jewels shone on her forehead. They were followed by the Chamberlain in his rich black cloak and bulbous hat. They all three stood smiling on the steps before the open doors. Inside the palace, servants and guards were gathered. The air was filled with excited murmurings and whisperings. What was to happen? Whatever it was, the people were sure it would be something to make them glad.

A very young herald blew his long thin horn, sounding a high note.

Cadfan stepped forward.

'His Royal Highness, Prince Madoc, has news for you. He asks you please to listen to what he has to say.'

The crowd stood still. No baby cried. Mordec saw that their raised faces were cheerful in expectation of his saying something to thrill them.

Cadfan bowed as he handed him the scroll. Mordec took off his glasses and handed them to Cadfan. He unrolled the scroll and read, in a loud clear voice, the large writing of the words that Angharad had composed for him.

When he had finished, he rolled up the scroll and, with his glasses back on, stood for a few moments looking from face to face of people in the crowd, people he had deceived for many days to their de-light! They look a little bewildered, uncertain, torn perhaps, Mordec guessed, between sorrow for his going and joy for his own joy.

Acting on a sudden impulse, Mordec held out his arms to them, holding the wound-up scroll tightly in his right hand, and spoke these words of his own:

'My dear people, I ask for your consent for me to go. I ask you please to send me on my way with your good will and kindness. I need to take your love with me, to keep me safe on this journey that I long to make, until I return to be your sovereign again.'

Then the crowd broke into loud cheers, young girls blew him kisses, laborers threw their hats in the air. Shouts of 'Long live Prince Madoc!', 'Come back safe!', 'We love you!' rang out.

Now horses were brought to the steps, two saddled and two laden with bundles. And the front two—a gleaming chestnut and a smaller grey, were being led by the Chief Huntsman.

'Fletch!' Mordec said, and stretched out his hand to him in the royal gesture that had become quite natural to him. Fletch bowed over it. But Mordec stepped forward and grasped his shoulder. 'My old friend,' he said, 'I'll miss you.'

Fletch swallowed the lump in his throat, and stepped back, reaching again for the horses' reins.

Leif appeared at Mordec's side in spruce scarlet livery. Tegwen rushed out of the palace and clasped his hand. She looked as if she had much to say, but before she could utter a word, Mordec kissed her cheek and murmured in her ear, 'Marry Cledwyn!' Then he embraced Angharad, Cadfan bowed to him, the very young herald blew his high note, and he and Leif mounted. Each took the reins in one hand and the lead of a pack horse in the other, and they started forward. The crowd parted to make way for them, still cheering.

Angharad and Cadfan watched them, more than a little sadly, until they were out of sight, Angharad waving, and Cadfan standing with one arm raised straight up, in a long-sustained farewell salute.

And that's how it came about that Mordec and Leif left the land of Owaindale mounted on fine geldings, with much money and treasure; and food and drink in gold and silver vessels, enough to see them comfortably supplied all the way to the ship that would take them home.

captain anwid has a great idea

Mark, King of Cornwall, had sought seclusion in his island castle after his beautiful young wife had vanished on the very night of their wedding. But then n a daughter of a distant relation on his mother's English side, his friend, Bummy of Felldown, with whom he had fenced and caroused in their wild youth, sent a plea from the mainland for a night's lodging, along with a letter from his old chum. The message came in the hand of a girl who, he was told, was waiting anxiously for an answer at the far end of the causeway, watching the tide come in. He at once sent word that as soon as she could cross to the island on dry sand, she and her retinue would be warmly welcomed as guests.

King Mark was not by nature gloomy. But he thought it the damnedest thing that a wife should disappear right after her wedding without a word of explanation or apology, and he couldn't help feeling depressed. He had turned fifty, and had been looking forward to the companionship of a woman in his later years. On top of that, the sheer mystery of how and why she had vanished teased his understanding.

'Company will do me good,' he told the few ladies and gentlemen of the court he had with him—to their pleasure, if also to their mild surprise. And he ordered a sumptuous dinner and asked Bruce, his ancient castellan, to accompany him to the cellars as he would choose the wines himself.

Though he was plainly doing his best to seem cheerful, Anwid found him—though certainly kind—a little distracted. She asked him if there was something weighing on his mind, and he replied yes, as a matter of fact, he had to admit, there was something.

After dinner, as the two of them reclined on long cushioned chairs, side by side, wrapped up in furs, watching through a triple-arched casement the white crests of dark waves, he told her what it was he sorrowed for.

When he had done, closing his sad tale with the words 'I loved her, you see,' she said nothing at first, but reached out and laid her hand on his for a few moments. Then she said, 'Cousin, Your Majesty, you are still a handsome man, and there are many lovely women in this big world. You will fall in love again. You will find a wife who will be true to you. But not if you shut yourself away in this remote keep. Return, I beg you, to Tintagel. Gather friends about you. Hold feasts, and dances, and jousts, and when summer comes, fill the nights with games and laughter. I promise that if you make merry, happiness will follow,'

'I might try that, cousin,' he said. 'But—whatever is that?'

They both leant forward as an apparition, lit by lantern-light streaming from a ring of little boats, arose out of the sea, a human form draped in sea-weed, with the head of a smiling dolphin and little turtles hung in rows along its arms. It twirled about, and sank, and the lights went out.

Aghast, King Mark turned to his companion.

'There is witchcraft at work,' he said hoarsely. 'Witchcraft! I hadn't thought of that. A curse has been put on me. My wife was bewitched away!'

But Anwid was laughing heartily. 'Be still, dear cousin,' she said. 'That is only a little dancer I brought with me. Charlotte is her name. She likes to entertain with little acts that make people gape. She does no harm. She was only tying to amaze and delight us.'

'And those,' the King said, pointing to the sea where the little boats had been, and where now, Anwid saw, other, much bigger boats were drifting in, on which men stood in black robes and black hoods, each carrying a lantern that lit his chin. 'Are those part of the entertainment?'

'No, no!' she said, rising to her feet. 'They have nothing to do with me. I did not bring those. But I think know who they are—'

'So do I,' Mark said. 'They are the black monks from the Abbey of de Llama, which sits on the island off the coast of France which is twin to this of mine. Now what can they want here, at this hour?'

He soon had his answer.

A monk was asking to speak with him, bringing a message from the Abbot.

'Come with me,' he said to Anwid, and she followed him to his throne room, where a servant was waiting to cloak him in ermine and put a narrow crown on his head and a sceptre in his hand. When he had seated himself on the strangely rough wooden throne, he asked Anwid to stand beside him, and he nodded at one of the knights in armour who had lined up along the walls to let the messenger in.

The black-clothed monk did not bow to the King. Nor did he put back his hood. He walked to the foot of the throne and spoke.

'I come in the name of our Holy Mother the Church,' he said, 'instructed by His Holiness the Pope and the faithful servant of Christ, Abbot Alonso de Llama. He asks that you permit a task force of our soldiers to search this island and the mainland that falls under your rule for persons wanted in connection with the dire crime of murder. We have reason to believe that the villain, a Viking whose name is Mordec, is in your realm, and if not he himself, his father whose name is Hauk.'

'Never heard of them,' the King said. 'What murder? When? What makes you think they are in Cornwall? Have you ever heard of them, cousin?' he asked, looking up at Anwid.

And it was right then that Anwid had her inspiration. She had been thinking, 'These men are rude. The Abbot is merciless. They may have brought soldiers with them, and in any case if they are armed they are too many for my gels to kill.'

'Why yes,' she said. 'As a matter of fact I do. At least I know where Mordec may be found. Of this Hauk I know nothing. But Mordec I saw with my own eyes only a few days ago.'

'And where was that?' the black monk demanded to know.

'At the Castle of Yggdrasil. I'm surprised you didn't think of looking there. It is a Viking castle, a short way north of London.'

The black monk bowed his head curtly to the King, turned about and bustled out.

Soon the boats were on their way, sailing north. The King and Anwid, back under furs, watched them go.

'Is he a very bad man, this Mordec?' the King asked. 'Do you know who it was he murdered, why and where and when?'

'He is not bad at all, 'Anwid replied. 'He is a dear good boy, just becoming a man, and he felled a villain who would have killed his friend with an axe. He did it to save his friend's life. The man he killed was a very bad man.'

'Then why did you give him away? They are going after him. They will capture him and bring him back for trial and condemn him. They are not merciful, I know full well.'

Anwid laughed again, that hearty laugh of hers. 'I have a joke to share with you, cousin,' she said. 'I have no notion where Mordec is. He is lost. He went adrift on my own ship, which I am seeking. I know where he is not, and that's the castle of Yggdrasil.'

'He's not there? So—why—I mean, what will happen when they get there and find they have been misled?'

'They will be slaughtered, every one.'

And when Anwid had finished describing what awaited them, the sort of welcome they would get from Embla and Askr, the King—though a kindly man—was laughing too, and for a little while he quite forgot his sorrow.

ships that pass in the night

Mordec and Leif caught up with the mule and cart train carrying Maradudd's copper to Sveinsey, and followed it to the wharf of the big, busy harbour.

The first thing Mordec did was to enquire if there were any Viking ships home-bound. There were none today, nor expected tomorrow, he was told. But the ship on which the copper was being loaded was bound for East Francia, stopping at five ports on the way.

'East Francia? That means it will pass near my home,' Mordec told Leif, unable to keep himself from smiling. 'So let's load ourselves on board along with the copper.'

He introduced himself to the Captain of the round ship as 'Mordec, legate of the royal house of Owaindale, travelling with one attendant'. The Captain, a big man with pale hair and beard, gave his name as Carolus. Mordec asked him how much he wanted to give them passage to East Francia. Captain Carolus looked the extraordinarily young legate up and down, priced in his mind the cost of the clothes he wore, and named a large fee.

Mordec took out his purse and counted gold and silver coins into the big hand held out to receive them.

'For this much I'll expect fine fare for me and my page,' he said. 'A hammock for me and a soft bed under it for him.'

'You'll get the best we have, Your Honour,' the Captain said, baring very white teeth between his yellow moustache and yellow beard.

'Will we and our baggage be safe on your ship? Are your men honest?' Mordec asked.

'I've been trusted with Owaindale copper for seven years,' the Captain said, 'and no one has complained of thievery.'

'Good,' Mordec replied. 'Now lend me a man to unload my baggage from the horses and stow it where I can get at it with ease.'

Mordec turned the horses over to the leader of the mule and cart train to be taken back to Owaindale. Then he and Leif went on board, where they were happy to find the Captain waiting to welcome them with cakes and ale.

They set out as soon as the high tide began to ebb, moving easily out of the harbour under full sail. The ship lay low in the water, heavy with its freight. The night was cold but the sky was clear, and a full moon rose over the western rim of the great Sea of Atlantis.

Leif attached himself to one of the sailors who had a small pet monkey called Pippin, and 'helped' him with his tasks, which meant that he chased the monkey halfway up the mast time and time again, until he and Pippin fell asleep in a huddle together on a heap of hides under the Captain's table.

Mordec swung in a hammock slung between a mast and the upturned serpent's tail of the figurehead. He gazed up at the moon, thinking of what he would do when he got home.

If he found out that his suspicions were true, that it was Gus who had shut him in the hold of the burning ship and left him there to die of suffocation or in flames, it would be for him to decide on what punishment his sometime friend should be sentenced to. What Gus had done was made worse by the fact that Mordec had saved his life. But then, it could be said that Mordec owed him that, because Gus had striven hard and successfully to help Queen Lily save him from being put to death for a crime he had not committed.

'I cannot decide now what I will do. I must first get home, get Gus to confess before the Thing, if what I suspect is true.'

And he fell into a deep and dreamless sleep as the ship sailed calmly west-south-west toward Land's End over the moonlit water.

* * *

Hauk could not sleep that night. He had convinced himself that he would find Mordec alive and well in Runnydale.

He lolled beside the crates on which Bjarwulf and Pelf sat and played hneftafl by moonlight or lanternlight, while Delfinola, cosy and grand in a sleeveless coat of pure white polar-bear fur, reclined in a gilded howdah with crimson curtains and cushions that

Pelf had selected from Bjarwulf's warehouse for the comfort of his wife on the voyage. Her curtains were open, she had a lantern of her own slung from the crossbeams of the contraption, and by its light she sewed warm woollen undergarments for her husband. She did not sing, because at the other end of the ship the Vikings were drinking and hollering, making far too much of a racket to let a man doze, even if Hauk had wanted to.

'Sail!' cried the lookout man high on the mast.

Out of habit, Bjarwulf and Pelf paused in their game and looked where the man was pointing.

'It's a round boat,' Bjarwulf said.

'Coming out of Sveinsey carrying copper, I expect,' said Pelf.

'Don't even think about it,' Hauk called to them.

'I wasn't …' Bjarwulf began.

'Oh yes you were,' Hauk said, laughing.

Pelf could not take his eyes off the ship, a black silhouette on the path of the moonlight. He moved close to Bjarwulf and whispered, 'I know it's copper. It would be the raid of the year.'

Bjarwulf turned his head away. 'You know I can't,' he said.

'A real pity' Pelf said. 'It would be our richest haul in two years. Not another sail in sight. It's not usually so empty on this sea-road. It would be easy …'

Bjarwulf, used to taking Pelf's advice, looked ruefully back at the tempting prey.

'No!' Hauk shouted, guessing what the whispering was about.

Reluctantly the captain and his accountant returned to the game.

'Well don't blame me,' Pelf said as he plonked himself down angrily on his crate, 'when the day comes …'

'When the day comes when we will all be looking back at what we could have done and did not do, when we will all be sighing for what will come to us no more, 'Delfiniola called lyrically into the night, 'then we will turn to sweeter things that are to be remembered, and sweeter yet that are to come.'

'Why yes, my love,' Pelf said. And he looked no more towards the ship on the path of the moonlight, which advanced and sailed by so close, Bjarwulf could calculate that his grappling hooks would reach the deck after but twenty strokes of the oars, and Hauk could see a man sleeping in a hammock.

'Sleep on in peace whoever you are,' Hauk said to him in his thoughts. 'You'll not be brought this night to death or slavery.'

So the ships glided past each other. Captain Carolus was relieved to see the Viking ship sail quietly on. The look of it had made him fear it was a pirate ship rather than a trader. He had gathered the crew amidships and was ready to distribute arms. Now the crew went back about its business.

And through it all, Leif had slept on in his soft bed, and Mordec in his hammock.

a disappointment

The rocks off the coast of Runnydale were far too many and dangerous to allow any boats except small fishing craft to be navigated to the shore. There was a small harbour for the fishing boats, whose owners were happy to carry goods and people between a trading vessel anchored beyond the high barrier of a rocky headland and the wooden jetty. (The Good Ship Good had landed on submerged rocks, and Mordec had waded ashore when the tide was out. A less sturdy ship would have been broken, but Captain Anwid's vessel did not even spring a leak, and floated out to sea again with its bottom intact when the tide came in.)

It was high noon when the Serpent King dropped anchor at a safe distance from the rocky headland.

Hauk protested at the dropping of the anchor that far from the shore.

'No, no—sail in, sail in,' Hauk impatiently urged the captain.

'Cannot,' Bjarwulf replied. 'Two dangerous even for my flat bottom.' Although he had never called there before, he was as aware of the hazards on that stretch of the coastline as was every Viking captain.

Hauk hailed one of the fishing boats. The two rowers came alongside the Serpent King.

'Will you take me ashore?' Hauk called to them. 'I have business there.'

'What business have you with us?' one of the fishermen called back, rising to his feet and cupping his hands in front of his mouth to help his voice carry. 'What are you trading?'

His companion pulled him down into the boat and began to turn and head back to shore.

'I've heard of you, Serpent King,' the second man shouted. 'You're no trader. You're a pirate. We'll not take pirates ashore. Better be on your way.'

'No, no!' Hauk shouted back. 'We come in peace. Please—come back!'

As the fishermen rowed on vigorously away from them, Hauk said, 'I'll swim, I'll wade, I'll climb ashore, whatever I must do …'

'Wait, my friend,' Bjarwulf said. 'Wait! They will tell their masters that we are here. Then we'll have ten boatfuls of armed men coming to see what we're all about—and *they'll* carry you ashore. Maybe in irons,' he guffawed, slapping Hauk on the back. Pelf, who stood on the other side of Bjarwulf looked round at Hauk's face—a picture of dismay—and joined in the laughter.

And sure enough, soon they came: not ten but seven boatfuls of armed coast guards, and Slate the Chief Runner in the leading boat. It was he who stood and hailed the Serpent King.

'This is the Coastguard of Runnydale. We would speak with the Captain of this ship!'

They watched a large man advance from amidships to the side. There were gold and silver rings in his ears and his nose, and a black horsetail sprouted from the top of his otherwise shaven head. He spread his feet wide apart, placed his thumbs in his broad belt and growled, 'I hear you. I am Captain Bjarwulf of the Serpent King.'

'Hail, Captain Bjarwulf! I am Slate, the chief officer of the Diarchy of Runnydale. I would talk with you, Captain. I ask to come aboard with my guards.'

'Not with all that company you don't.' the Captain replied firmly. 'You can come aboard alone.'

'If I come alone what protection will I have? There is talk in the harbour that you are a pirate.'

'That I might be,' Bjarwulf conceded, somewhat chuffed that even in this small piece of the world he was recognized and that his reputation went before him. 'But I'm not here to do my usual work. I'm looking for a lost Viking.'

'I thought you might be. And I wish to help you.'

At this point, Hauk, who had been standing back while the two men sounded each other out, rushed forward and cried out, 'Honoured chief, if you have news of a lost Viking boy named Mordec, I beg you tell me—I am his father.'

Slate saw how earnest this milder Viking looked, heard how fervently he pleaded, and decided he would be safe if he went aboard alone—with the precious information he had to give him.

'I have more to tell than I can shout from a rocking boat. Convince me that I have nothing to fear from you. What can I depend on—in addition to keeping my guards close to your ship ready to board if I shout for them?'

'Why sure, you will be safe as a babe in its mother's arms,' came the sweet tones of Delfinola. Gently pushing Hauk and Bjarwulf apart, she took up a commanding position between them, stretched out her arms towards Slate and crooned, 'How would you not be most welcome, noble chief? Come aboard our ship, share with us a flagon of our golden mead, and tell us—sad seekers who have wandered on barren shores and braved tempest and angry seas in search of our darling lost boy—what news you have of him.'

Slate stared for a few moment at the strange figure, so tall, so narrow, her long white hair, her face not young yet not without beauty, her bright eyes imploring him as a heroine in a legend would implore a knight to aid her, and he could no more refuse her request than he could have openly defied his sovereign lords.

Bjarwulf, Pelf, Hakon and Gus stated their names to Slate. He nodded to each one in what he hoped was a reassuringly friendly manner. Then they all sat in a circle on the deck, Hauk facing Slate, while a smiling Delfinola brought them cockles in shells and mead in beakers, and Slate began to tell them what he knew about Mordec; that he had been found on Runnydale's shore, been kindly cared for, given shelter and food and clothing; that he remembered escaping from confinement on an abandoned ship that had for a short time been set on fire ... and ...

Gus tipped his head back as if to look at the sky but he closed his eyes and his face reddened.

Hauk, who had found it hard to contain his impatience, broke into Slate's story to ask, breathlessly, 'So he's here? He's safe, and well, and somewhere near by?'

Slate shook his head, but also held up a hand and said quickly, 'No but he's free, he's on his way home.'

'Not here? On his way home? How? When?'

'All your questions will be answered if you'll let me go on,' Slate said, casting a sidelong glance at Bjarwulf. The Captain kept his eyes steadily on the stranger's face even while taking a long swallow from the very large goblet he reserved for his personal use.

Slate took silence to mean assent, and went on to tell how he had set Mordec on the long road home.

'… And,' he concluded his narrative, 'I saw them start off, up the mountain path, warmly clad, well supplied with meat and bread …'

'Them?' said Hauk. 'Why do you say them? Was there someone with him?'

'A boy,' Slate said. 'A younger boy. A Viking boy. Another lost Viking boy. Leif is his name.'

'Leif,' Hauk repeated. He touched his purse where the talisman lay that the Skald's daughter had given him to bring him luck, a bracelet with a silver link, and the name 'Leif' cut into it. His thoughts were spinning. His enormous relief on hearing that Mordec had indeed survived the burning ship was matched by bitter disappointment that he was not here.

Gus, frowning, asked Slate, 'But why didn't you put them on a ship? Any ship?'

'Few ships call here. Weeks go by and no ship calls. Few have a reason to. We have no port, only a little fishing harbour. It's rare for a traveler to come to us. We need few things from other lands. We grow or make what we need, mostly. If I'd waited for a ship it might have been too late.'

'Why too late? Too late for what? What might have happened if you'd waited?'

Hauk longed to pull all the answers at once out of this cautious Welshman who knew so much and answered so slowly.

Slate hesitated, and Bjarwulf's eyes narrowed suspiciously.

'Were you scared?' he asked. 'Scared that if you didn't get rid of him quick Vikings might descend on your nice little country and plunder it dry, and lay it waste, and leave every man with his ribs spread out like bony wings?'

This time Slate replied at once. 'I hope you understand that I did my best for your boy. Your boys. I cared for them. I befriended them. I am your friend. I have proved it.'

'I understand that,' Hauk said, 'and I thank you for it. We—we thank you for it.' He looked round the circle. Hakon and Gus nodded, Bjjarwulf grunted and took a noisy suck from his beaker.

'But, if you please,' Hauk went on, 'tell me what you fear would have happened if you had waited to put them on a ship?'

Slate swallowed. He had hoped to avoid that question. At last he said, 'Hear me. I hope for your understanding. I am a loyal servant of my two masters, the

Lord Humfrey and the Lord Alger. I obey them. If they had ordered that Mordec be held in captivity, I would have obeyed that order. Do you follow me?'

'You are telling me that you sent Mordec out of your country before such an order had been given? But that you expected it to be given?'

'My Lords are good men. I do not disobey them. I do as they say and I do not ask why …'

'But you thought that they …' Hauk began.

'Or perhaps just one of them …' Slate put in.

'Might give such an order and …'

'And then you feared that the fury of the Northmen would descend on you,' Bjarwulf growled in his most threatening manner.

'I did, Captain.' Slate said. 'I did.'

Hakon wiped the mead from his yellow moustache with the back of his hand and then, clutching his ample beard, spoke up. 'Couldn't you explain that good reason to your masters?' he asked. 'Wouldn't they see the soundness of it?'

'It is a strange thing,' Slate said, 'But though my two masters have ruled this small country for twenty years, and the country has run smoothly in peace and happiness, the fact is, they have never agreed with each other. Both of course have good sense. Both have sound reasons for what they decree. But—but they never desire the same thing. If one says yes, the other says no. It is my job to find ways to …'

'To do what's needed no matter what either of them says?' Hauk said, and he could not restrain a brief wry smile.

'Yes, just so. Without ever going against the will of either of them. Just seeking …'

'A third way?' Hauk suggested.

Slate let out a long breath of relief. 'That's it,' he said. 'I don't suggest a way. I …'

'*Find* a way,' Hauk said. And he looked at Slate with new respect. This, he thought, is a clever and competent man. 'And I suppose you would rather your masters do not know that the boy's flight was in any way … er … eased … by your … er … acting in the best interests of your country?'

Slate nodded rapidly. 'Yes. Yes. Right. Exactly right. 'he said, 'I—I am grateful for your complete understanding and … and your discretion?'

'Can't say I understand it,' Bjarwulf said. 'Sounds crazy to me.'

He turned to Hauk.

'So what now?' he asked. 'The boy's on his way home. Maybe even there. We can start home too—and do a little business on the way.'

Slate rose. 'You will be needing fresh water. And supplies. We can sell you fine cured hams, and harps and trumpets.'

'Sell?' said Bjarwulf.

'Sell,' said Hauk firmly.

'And there's one thing more I could tell you,' Slate said, rising. 'But I want an—an agreement, an—an understanding with you *all* …' he looked straight at Bjarwulf, who dropped his chin into his beard and his eyes to the deck, 'that we, the people of Runnydale, freely giving our friendship to you and your kin, receive your friendship in return, your friendship and goodwill—for all time?'

'For all time?' said Pelf.

And Bjarwulf echoed, '*For all time?*', lifting his head and his bushy eyebrows in amazement.

'Why yes,' said Slate.

'Yes,' said Hauk, also rising. 'It is agreed. We all agree, don't we?'

Hakon and Gus rose and nodded. Bjarwulf followed, and then Pelf. One by one they gripped the Welshman's forearm as he gripped theirs, in the style the world had learnt from the Romans.

'What is this one thing more you have to tell us?' Hauk prompted him.

'If you, Hauk, will come ashore,' Slate said,' and dine with me in my house tonight, I will explain. I'll send a boat at sunset to bring you in.'

With that he turned abruptly, marched to the side of the Serpent King, climbed over and dropped into a boatful of coastguards waiting for him.

'Pull,' he ordered the rowers as soon as he was seated. He looked back at the faces of the Vikings, all lined up and watching him depart, and he raised one arm in a friendly salute. The men returned it. And Delfinola, leaning over, put both her hands to her lips and then spread them out to imply a scattering of kisses. Then she waved, and smiled, and shouted, 'We part only to meet again, dear new friend!'

Slate smiled back, waved back, but did not think it would be dignified to blow kisses.

'Will you come to dine with me too, lady?' he called.

'Oh yes,' she cried. 'I will come, I will come, and he will come with me.' She pointed a forefinger down towards Pelf's head.

Slate turned to face the harbour, and became thoughtful. He had never planned to join his life with a woman's, but if *that* woman …

He shook his head and dismissed the idea from what was, after all, his very practical mind.

slate owns up to his masters

Slate went first to the sterner of his two masters, who, he knew, would be in his workroom. The Runner at the door took in his request to be admitted at once on urgent business.

'Is that you, Slate?' Lord Humfrey called. 'You can come in. Did you say it was about something urgent?'

'Yes, my lord, I asked to see you urgently.' Slate said as he stepped inside. The Runner went out and closed the door behind him.

'Don't like the sound of it,' Humfrey said, putting down the tool with which he was working on a model of a wheeled ship that could be rowed over land as well as in water.

'Everything's all right, my lord,' Slate said hastily. 'I have dealt with it. I've come to apologize for not seeking your orders before I acted, and to tell you what I have done and why I had to act quickly.'

'So it's not urgent any more?'

'Only urgent that you become informed, my lord,' Slate said.

'Have you told *him* about whatever it is?'

He meant his fellow ruler, Alger, of course. Neither of them used the other's name if he could avoid it.

'Not yet, my lord, I came to you first.'

'Ah, very good, I'm listening.'

'My lord—it's some Vikings. Dropped anchor near the harbour. But we—

'Vikings? Traders or raiders?'

'We are safe, my lord, as safe as if they were a shipful of lambs. I assure you. They are full of goodwill towards us. Let me tell you what I have done, and I think you will agree that I acted well—very well.'

'You didn't promise them payoff?'

'No, my lord, nothing like that. What I did was—you remember the Viking boys who … escaped? Well, they've come looking for them. So—you will understand why, my lord, I had to do it—I told them a lie. I not only told them that we had looked after the boys, I also told them *that I had helped them escape*. I said that I gave them sacks of food and showed them the safe path up the mountain. I said I did it without letting my masters know. And, my lord—this, ha-ha, you'll like this, this is the best part—they are *very grateful to me*. They say they're in my everlasting debt. Well, they say that they'll be in my everlasting debt if the boys get home safe and well. Anyway, they are not going to do a thing to harm us. No raiding, no plundering—and if the boys get home safely, they'll put the word about among the Northmen that Runnydale *is an ally and friend*. I told them I'd think of a way to explain to my masters how that comes to be—but in fact of course I can simply tell you the truth. That I lied to them. I took my life in my hands and went to them. They had me on board. They gave me mead and cockles. There was a woman … never mind that. I talked to them, and we drank, and we parted friends. I think I have done good for Runnydale this day, my lord.'

Humfrey was silent for a few moments as he mulled over what he'd been told.

'You told them you'd *helped* the boys escape?'

'I did, my lord, and hope that you'll forgive me for telling an untruth'

Humfrey laughed, only briefly, but even a brief laugh was more than he usually gave in to.

Slate smiled, nodded, and felt relieved.

'I thought, my lord, I'd *set* the friendship by letting one or two of them land and dine at my house—with your permission.'

'I wouldn't trust a Viking too far, whatever he promises,' Humfrey said. 'Have Runners stay close. Swords, bows, spears.'

'I will, my lord.'

'So now you'll go and tell *him*? You won't find it easy to make him understand. He doesn't grasp things quickly. And it's all rather hard to understand, anyway. But persevere, persevere.'

'You wouldn't want me to bring the Vikings to you?'

'No. The time may come for ruler to meet ruler in a real alliance with the Northmen, but that time is not now. Keep them grateful to you. Watch them carefully.'

'Yes, my lord. Thank you for your advice.'

As Slate expected, the Lord Alger was lolling in his garden on a large tawny dog and some cushions made of white bear fur by a round pool where tiny fat red fishes swam.

Into the pool a zestful brook ran down and entered pipes which bore its water up through the statue of a boy, to trickle out through his pursed lips and fall tinkling back on to the surface, where now and then a red fish mouth appeared to gulp a falling drop.

It was an unseasonably warm day for early spring. Sunlight fell on clumps of daffodils in bloom. The Lord Alger's beloved peacocks trailed their glorious tails across the greensward.

Three attendants, identical triplet brothers dressed in daffodil yellow, plucked the strings of gilded harps.

'Ah, Slate, my good fellow,' Alger called cheerfully. 'What news? Come and sit with us and tell us how the world goes.'

The black rubbery lips of the dog blew out and in twice, as the animal made a lazy attempt at a growl.

Slate ignored it.

'I do have news,' Slate said, smiling.

He perched on the stone balustrade that circled the pool.

'A Viking ship has anchored near the harbour. I've dealt with it. No worries.'

'A Viking ship, eh? Haven't seen one of those for months. Just the one? How many on board? You've spoken to them? What do they want?' Alger stayed in his comfortable position. No look of concern crossed his smooth close-shaven face. Only his voice hinted at a touch of anxiety.

'They're looking for the boy, Mordec. They asked have we seen him.'

'And what did you tell them?'

'I told them he'd been here. I said we looked after him well. Fed him. Gave him clothes because his own were in tatters. I said we asked him to stay but he wanted to try and get home.'

'Have they gone?'

'Not yet. I asked one or two of them—tamer looking types—to dine with me tonight. And there's a woman with them, Irish I think. They mean no harm.'

'You're letting them into your house? They'll help themselves to whatever they want.'

'I don't think they will, my lord. I made them feel grateful to me. I even said I'd given Mordec food for his journey and shown him the safe path up the mountain.'

'And they believed you?'

'I think so, yes. I said we've never been enemies of the Northmen, and would like to be friends. I said we'd like to trade with them regularly if only we had a good harbour …'

'Not having a good harbour keeps us safe. You never know when Viking traders will turn into raiders. In the wink of an eye it can happen. I must warn you, you are taking a risk. Double the number of Runners on guard, and tell the boatmen to carry only the ones you've invited to the shore.'

'Would you care to meet them, my lord?'

Alger stroked the dog's head slowly as he considered if he did.

'No,' he said at last. 'Vikings don't appeal to me. They're alright when they're very young, like Mordec and Leif, but the big ones are uncouth.'

Alger's hand shifted to the bearskin rug and stroked it with the same gentle movement as had soothed the dog.

'Did they ask about Leif too?'

'No. I told them he went with Mordec, but they didn't seem to know anything about him.'

'Did you tell them how they came to be here?'

'Briefly. How we found Mordec. I thought I'd ask Zarath to come and tell them about the Granting.'

'Have you told *him*?' Alger murmured.

'The Lord Humfrey knows what I have done and what I plan to do this evening.'

'He's not too pleased about it, eh?'

'No he's not pleased, but he's leaving it to me to do the right thing.'

'Have a nice evening,' Alger said.

With that, Slate knew, he was dismissed. He bowed to Alger and waved one sweeping wave to all three of the brothers, whose hands continued without pause to stray over the harp strings as indolently as Alger's hand stroked his live dog and his dead bear.

slate's dinner party

This is what Slate's Belgian cook prepared for the dinner-party: salmon sizzled in butter, seasalt, and grated ginger root; roasted shark wrapped in caramelized leeks; seabass in applesauce and basil; broiled duck legs threaded with fried bacon; smoked ham rolled in honey and rhubarb; ham with gooseberry sauce; pigeon breasts and yellow pears stewed in blackberry wine; black cherry cake with whipped cream stained black with octopus ink.

And Slate brought up six flagons of Samian wine from his cool cellar. He had bought them from a curly-haired Greek merchant and explorer whose blue ship with a blue sail had anchored once only, some three years earlier, off Runnydale's shore. The Greek had told him it was the most famously wonderful wine in the world, that ballads had been written in its honour—one of which he sang on the jetty to Slate, some coast guards, and the fishwives who gutted fish for the market. He had then let Slate taste the wine, and Slate had granted that for once a salesman was probably telling the truth about his merchandise.

The Lord Alger had bought the greater part of the wine cargo, and the Greek had bought five gilded harps for a third of what he'd demanded and been paid in all for the wine, and had sailed away with three of the younger Runners on board, who had not as yet returned.

Slate had kept his flagons for a special occasion, which was what tonight's dinner party was. Of course this wine was not something that rough Vikings like Bjarwulf and Hakon would have a taste for, but they were not coming. It would surely not be wasted on Hauk, whose beard was neatly trimmed and who was, after all, a meadmaker and a sort of tavern keeper.

And the Princess was coming, and she knew what fine things were. When she had first arrived, Slate had thought her gross, but she had become less so, and he had come to like her.

She had sat with him in his garden and confided in him that she had always been unhappy until she had come to 'this little paradise' and met the great Zarath, of whom she had heard since her childhood. She had asked him if he could use his magic to make her happier.

'And could he? Did he?' Slate had asked.

'Oh, yes!' she said. 'He gave me certain herbs that I had to chew three times every day. And for them to work properly I had to fast every second day. And every morning in the first light of dawn, I had to rise from my bed and run round the palace three times, reciting certain spells, which I cannot tell you because they must remain secret. I became quite hungry, yet also, definitely, happier. And I'll tell you something else he did. He spread the hot wax of candles on my face, to bring out my beauty he said. All it seemed to bring out was hair. Right out it came, stuck to the wax. But he told me that's how the magic worked.'

Slate had his own idea as to why the Princess, no longer as large as when she had first arrived, nor as hairy in the face, was happier, and he didn't put it all down to mysterious herbs and magic spells—though his respect for Zarath, already high, had risen a little higher, not despite but because of his little deceptions.

One day, as they had sat talking in his garden, she had mentioned to him that she remembered meeting the Viking boy Mordec in Italy. She had said no more about it, but Slate was sure that Hauk would be glad to hear about it. This was 'the thing' he'd promised Hauk would please him.

'The father of Mordec has arrived on a ship searching for him,' he told the Princess when he went to her richly appointed quarters to invite her to his dinner party. 'Will you tell him how you met Mordec in Italy?'

'I will,' she said. 'Will Zarath be there?'

Yes, Zarath had agreed to come too. A much-travelled man of great renown, he would likely have heard of the wine, perhaps had drunk it, and even perhaps had heard a ballad or two sung in its honour.

And Slate had a favor to ask of him too.

'Will you tell the father of Mordec about the Granting? I mean, the real story of how you found the boy—and then—well, what you did.'

'It might not be what he would like to hear,' Zarath said dubiously, thinking of the sleeping draught he had administered to the weary boy to keep him quiet until the moment he would be 'magicked' into existence in front of a thousand eyes.

'I think he would like to hear it,' Slate said firmly. 'All of it.'

Zarath sighed. 'Very well,' he promised.

And then, also, there would be the Lady Delfinola, escorted, quite unnecessarily, by the short Viking man. And, well, sooth to say, the wine was brought up from the cellar chiefly for her.

Slate sent a Runner to tell the gardener to bring in pots of hyacinths so the air of the dining-hall would be sweet with their perfume. He had one of the pots, with three blooms, pink, white, and blue, placed in the middle of the dining-table.

'She will like that,' Slate murmured to himself, picturing Delfinola sitting beside him, breathing in the fragrance of the flowers, smiling, sipping the beautiful golden wine, her long white hair shining in the soft light of wax candles.

On entering Slate's dining-hall, to the door of which Dave the Fisher led the foreign guests, the short thin-haired accountant Pelf looked all round him, his glance darting here and there even while he returned the bow of his host. 'Assessing the value of my possessions,' Slate thought, though he went on smiling pleasantly.

There were Runners posted round the hall as well as at the doors, instructed to make sure that if the Vikings gave way to their instincts and seized things—the candelabra, the pewter plates and jugs, the tapestries, or the tempting shields, bows, swords and spears arranged ornamentally on one of the walls—they would not take them far.

He expected the two Vikings to be armed, but Pelf seemed not to be. And Hauk came dressed in a white tunic that could not easily conceal a weapon if he'd been carrying one.

True, the Lady Delfinola had a dagger in the sea-green sash round the waist of her seagreen gown, but it was so richly jewelled that Slate believed she had placed it there purely for ornament.

Zarath and the Princess were already in the room when the doors were opened by the Runners and the visitors from the Serpent King entered, Delfinola smiling upon Slate, touching his outstretched hand lightly with her own and murmuring, 'Dear, dear man!'

Slate proudly presented them to 'the Princess Starling' and 'the famous Magician, Zarath of the East'.

Hauk bowed.

Pelf ran his eye over their ornaments. He reckoned the ruby ring on the Princess's finger and the gold chain round Zarath's neck were together worth half the price of a ship.

Delfinola clasped her hands together. 'Ah, royal lady, I am a child of Good Fortune, raised for this moment, this happiness, to come together with Your Highness at this hour in this place of all the places in all the world.'

She reached for the Princess's hand—the one without the ring on it—and lightly kissed it. Then she took Zarath's hand in both of hers, and holding it gently as one would a delicate bird, sighed and declared, 'And to find myself too in the presence of Magic, the person himself whom the world will forever remember and celebrate. Have I not, from this day, been enchanted by your touch.' She let go and curtsied slowly and gracefully.

Slate had not been able to take his eyes off her. Recollecting where he was and what he should be doing, he ushered her to the chair beside his own.

And so it happened just as he had hoped it would: the Lady Delfinola sitting beside him, her long white hair shining in the soft light of the candles. And she was speaking to him sweetly in her lovely voice.

She excused the absence of Bjarwulf: 'The darling man,' she said, in tones that made it seem to Slate she was singing even though she wasn't, 'so fearful he is to leave his ship. He loves every beam, and has it in his troubled head that all the world covets it, and if he leaves it for an hour it will be taken from him by jealous men, never to be found again. Ah, but he was torn between wishing to adventure in your green and kindly land and guarding his heart's love. And full of sorrow he was when he knew the adventure could not be. All this he tasked me to tell you, and faithfully I bring the words to you as he spoke them.'

As Slate had not invited Bjarwulf, the apology (which it was, of a sort) was unnecessary; and Slate could not suppress a doubt that Bjarwulf had used those words; but he truthfully told the lady, the main thing was that she had come.

The Princess seated herself next to Zarath, and praised the wine without being asked, to Slate's satisfaction.

While everyone was still sober, it was the Princess who set a friendly tone of easy talk.

'I understand from Chief Slate,' she said, looking at Hauk who was seated across the table from her, 'that you are the father of Mordec?'

'You knew him?' Hauk asked eagerly.

'I knew him even before we met in this little heaven of a place,' the Princess said. 'I met him first in Italy.'

'Where? How?'

Hauk gave all his attention to her story of Mordec and another boy—'who had lovely yellow hair'—appearing unexpectedly in her wagon when it was stationed for a night near Genova. She had no idea (she said) why they had entered her wagon. Either she did not recall that they had come looking for an English Queen whom she was just then holding bound and hidden, having been paid to do so by the very man who held her mother in his prison or his arms, or she chose to leave that part out. She and her attendant maidens, she said, had welcomed them and regaled them with rare delicacies. She had invited them to stay the night in the comfort of her wagon, and (she lied) they had fallen asleep on the cushions. 'I'll never forget the brightness of that yellow hair on the crimson silk,' she claimed. She was desolate when she found them gone in the morning. (Not a word did she say about giving them the choice between leaving her wagon immediately or being forced to stay with her forever.)

Zarath and Slate listened to the tale as attentively as Hauk did. Zarath welcomed all reports of events that came to him from anywhere and stored them in his prodigious memory. He knew better than to believe all that the story-teller alleged, but reckoned it was true that Mordec had been in Italy in the company of another Viking boy, and had encountered the Princess.

Slate guessed that the boy with the yellow hair was the very one who was at that moment on a ship off Runnydale's shore. He wondered what the real story was of his sojourn in Italy with Mordec.

Hauk too suspected that there was more to the story than the Princess had cared to tell, but he knew he would hear the truth from Mordec himself. So he thanked her and asked no more questions.

He turned back to Slate.

'You said you would tell me this evening how Mordec came to Runnydale, and what happened to him while he was here?'

'Zarath?' Slate prompted the Magician.

Zarath plunged into the story.

'Dave the Fisher found him asleep on the shore. He must have waded ashore at low tide from the ship that brought him here. He fetched me, and your boy woke when I roused him. He told me his name and asked me where he was. I told him this was Runnydale, and Dave and I led him to the shed where the fishwives gut and clean the fish. It was empty that day, because it was a special day. I was to give a performance of magic in the great hall of the palace in the evening, and I worked out a trick that would involve making your boy appear suddenly. I wanted him to sleep until I woke him that night in front of the folk and the Rulers, as the granting of a wish to the young Viking orphan boy who had some years ago come mysteriously to live among us. The boy would ask me to give him a Viking friend. He would ask for this as if it was entirely his own idea, you understand?'

Hauk nodded. 'Go on,' he said.

'Well, Mordec wanted a drink and I gave him a sleeping-draught. It had a good taste. And it was not harmful. Giving him just the right dose so he would wake when I needed him to—that was the hard part. But I got it right. He slept for hours on a bed of furs, and once he had woken in the great hall, and the folk had made sure he was a real live Viking I had brought magically into existence for the little orphan, the Runners took charge of him. He lived and ate and slept in their barn. He did not remember how he had come to be on our beach. He never did remember that while he was here. Or so he said. He remembered being in Italy, though he said no more about it than just that. He never mentioned meeting the Princess, but she says they did recognize each other. Slate will have told you the rest.'

Hauk believed him. If he felt any anger that his son had been drugged and used as a prop for a Magician's act, he did not let it show. He had questions to ask, but now, after Zarath's short tale was told, and every dish had been savored by everyone, and all the delicious wine had been drunk, everything began to appear a little hazy to them all.

Delfinola broke off the flowery tops of the hyacinth plants and delicately nibbled the little pink, white, and blue bells off their thick green stems, which she then laid down neatly beside the picked bone of a duck leg on her plate.

Slate, gazing into her shining eyes though he saw them through a golden mist, confessed that he worshipped her, and without having planned to do any such thing, he said, 'I offer you my heart, forever, dearest Delfinola.'

He listened to her reply as if to the sound of harps and the singing of choirs, and drunk though he was, her words lodged in his memory: 'Oh, darling man, so good and giving, whose sweet face I'll not forget in all my years to come, how warmly your loving words flow to my heart, like slow warm honey through my veins. Never will I forget you, nor will you lose the memory of me. And though we are doomed to part, and many a tide must rise and fall between us twain, this bond like none other will abide. It will abide.'

And then she was gone. Dave the Fisher had come to take her and the Vikings back to their ship. Slate was always to remember her long silvery white hair hanging down her back over the seagreen of her gown as she drifted away, her hand on the arm of the accountant. And he was not sure, and never would be sure, if he had proposed marriage to her; or whether, if he had, she had accepted his proposal.

He went to bed feeling he had done some good this day, but woke late in the night and remembered that Hauk had come to him and asked him which way Mordec would have gone once he had crossed over the mountain, and that he had not been able to speak but had waved his hand towards Zarath and murmured, or tried to murmur, 'Ask the Magician.'

And he thought, but wasn't sure, that one of his Runners had helped him to bed, pulled off his boots and pulled the bedclothes over him.

'She loves me,' he told the roof beams. 'She loves me, but we are doomed to part.'

He slept again, and found, when he woke in the morning, that all her words came back to him. He repeated them to himself now and then through his busy day. And every night, for the rest of his life, he said them over to himself when he first closed his eyes to sleep.

* * *

The Serpent King did not leave in the calm of the early morning, as its captain had intended. Hauk needed an hour or two ashore.

And when a fisherman responded to Hauk's shout and rowed up beside the Serpent King to ferry him ashore, Gus too dropped into the small boat.

'I want to find out more about what happened to Mordec while he was here,' he explained. Hauk understood his need, and together they landed again on the jetty of the little harbour. But there they parted. Hauk asked the way to Zarath's abode. Gus went a different way.

'Meet me back here at noon,' Hauk called after him. Gus waved to show he had heard, but did not turn round. The way he marched told Hauk that he had a plan of some sort he was anxious and determined to fulfill.

Zarath himself answered the knock on his front door. He had been expecting Hauk's visit. He led the way up the winding stairs to the room where he had listened to Mordec's questions and given his discouraging replies. Which he now regretted.

When he had heard of the 'escape', he alone, it seemed, doubted that it was the true or entire explanation of Mordec's sudden disappearance. He now thought he had been wrong to put his good standing with the Rulers ahead of the boy's desperate desire to return home.

'After all,' he argued to himself, 'they believe in my powers and would not willingly risk my enmity.'

Hauk said, 'Slate thinks you could tell me what I need to know.'

'Yes,' Zarath said, seating himself on his throne-like chair. 'I expected you to bring me questions.'

'It seems,' Hauk said, 'that Mordec was helped to leave Runnydale by way of a path over the eastern mountains. What I want to know is, how might he have made his way from there? What is the most likely way that someone on foot might go?'

Zarath rose and unrolled a chart on his table. He placed a pewter plate, a glass goblet, an abacus and a sleeping hedgehog on the four corners to keep it flat. Hauk came and stood beside him.

'Not eastward,' Zarath said. He pointed to a shaded area on the chart. 'There are more and higher mountains to the east. He would surely walk this way, south down the valley between the ranges, until he came again to the seashore, here. From there he would have an easier way to the port of Sveinsey down here, where he could find a Viking ship, or board any ship bound for northern parts that would take him on as a rower.'

There flashed before Hauk's inner eye a picture of the ship they passed soon after they rounded Land's End, that Bjarwulf had said was no doubt laden with copper it had taken on in the port of Sveinsey. That man asleep in a hammock on the deck—could he have been Mordec, he wondered. But at once he told himself, no. Rowers working their passage did not loll in hammocks like lords.

'He had a companion with him. Would the food they could carry last them through the long walk to Sveinsey?'

'They would most likely stop on the way to work for food. The only place they could have done that would be the Princedom of Owaindale, here.'

'Do you know anything about the Viking child who was with him? How he came to Runnydale?'

'He came as an infant. A fishwife brought him to the palace. She said a Spanish woman had handed him down to her husband from a ship that had anchored to unload cargo. The boy could tell us his name, but little more. The Rulers said he was to be fed and clothed and sent to school. Slate and his Runners looked after him in a casual sort of way. I think he was happy here. But the Runnydale boys did not take to him. He was lonely. I know this because he really did ask me if I could get him a friend. So when we found Mordec asleep on the beach …'

And now Zarath told Hauk about the annual Granting, and what happened at the last one. He described in detail what he did, neither claiming nor denying his magic powers. He ended by saying, 'There is more than a chance that your son and Leif are well on their way home—even perhaps already there. My advice to you is, go back. If he's not there yet, wait. From all I hear of him from the Princess, I suppose him to be a young man who can find his way in the world.'

'If he is home—or gets home before me—he and my wife will be … Oh, if only there was a way to let them know I am sailing home!'

Zarath lifted the plate, the goblet, the abacus and the hedgehog off the chart, rolled it up, thinking all the while. Finally he looked straight at Hauk and said, 'Perhaps there is a way. Come.'

He led Hauk up the winding stairs to the top of his tower, and there Hauk saw the pigeons housed in the brick wall with its many holes lined with straw.

Zarath took one of the birds gently in his hands.

'Some of them home to Julius the Troll who lives in the Northlands.'

'I know him!' Hauk exclaimed with rising excitement. 'He knows me, he knows my house, he knows

Mordec. If he got news of me he would send it on to my wife. He is a good Troll, and a clever one.'

'He is,' Zarath agreed. 'Here are small parchments and ink and a pen. Write your message.'

Hauk had begun eagerly to write when a new thought struck him.

'But if you had this … I mean—why …'

Zarath cut him short. 'You want to know why I didn't use this method of sending news to you that Mordec was here? I should have. I was wrong not to. I'm sorry I didn't. The Rulers wanted to keep him here. I did not want to go against their wishes. I ask your forgiveness.'

'You have it,' Hauk said. 'Since you are making amends now.'

Hauk watched while Zarath attached the parchments to the legs of two pigeons. To his surprise the Magician then put them back in their holes.

'I cannot release them now,' he explained. 'I have first to ask Slate to tie up his falcons that hunt pigeons for his table. They will go before evening.'

When Hauk reached the harbour he found Gus already there, talking to a Runner whose name, Gus told him, was Flint.

Flint said, 'So you are the father of Mordec?'

Gus said, 'Flint and the other Runners—they were good to Mordec. Flint has shown me the barn where they all slept, where Mordec slept. They gave him food, they gave him a cloak.'

Hauk put out his hand to Flint, and the two men clasped each other's forearms. Then Hauk took out his purse, and put a gold coin in Flint's palm, on which Flint closed his fingers, grinning.

'We think Vikings might come and take our gold, not give it to us,' he said.

'Can we get back quickly to the ship, please,' Gus said. He had been nervously looking about him. 'A woman has been chasing me ever since I passed the gates of the palace on the way here. She called me "Yellow-hair". I had to hide from her. She kept calling out that she was the Princess Starling. I remember meeting a Princess Starling in Italy, but she was a very fat woman with a hairy face, not like this one. I don't know what she wants of me, and I don't want to find out.'

As soon as they were back on the Serpent King, the anchor was raised, Lars and the crew hoisted the sail, a fair wind filled it, and soon Bjarwulf was steering the ship due north.

As the coast of Runnydale receded, Hauk told Gus what he had learned from Zarath, and how a message was on its way to Estrid, and possibly to Mordec who could be 'home or nearly home', he said.

On hearing Hauk say that, Gus did something that Vikings did not often do.

He wept.

He could not restrain tears of sheer relief.

And Hauk quietly, tactfully, walked away.

eyrin's surprise

Eyrin son of Hauk was in the orchard talking to the bees when a tall stranger in kingly clothes and eyeglasses pushed the gate open and walked straight up to him, smiling, then picked him up and held him high. Eyrin struggled in the stranger's grasp, shouting, 'Put me down! Help! Help! Mama!'

His mother Estrid came running from the house. 'What's going on? What's wrong? Eyrin, who—'

The king person put Eyrin down and ran to her, with his arms spread wide. A moment later he was holding her in a tight embrace. And she was both laughing and crying.

'Let her go! Let her go!' Eyrin screamed, kicking at the brute's legs in their high leather boots all smooth and shiny.

But he kept a tight hold of her, though her tears were falling. And though her tears were falling, she was laughing!

She pushed her head back and look up at the king person, smiling, and crying—or laughing—and she called out, 'Eyrin, come here, it's your brother. It's Mordec. He's here. He's come home!'

Mordec? This was Mordec? The big brother who was always going off somewhere when I wanted to play with him? Who taught me how to swim? And how to row my boat? And …

Eyrin went and peered up at the king person's face, which—yes, he thought—was a bit like Mordec's used to be. But the eyeglasses were different.

'Are you Mordec?' he asked. 'Why are you dressed like a king? Where have you been? Have you become a king?'

'In a way,' Mordec said. 'I was a sort of king for a time. I have lots of true stories to tell you. And I've brought kingly things home. Come and see.'

Again he picked up Eyrin, put an arm round Estrid's shoulders and took them to the gate. There Eyrin saw three shining chestnut brown horses, two of them laden with barrels and bundles, and a shaggy grey-and-white pony just like his own pony Snorri, which mother sat him on and led round the meadows. On this one sat a boy a few years older than himself, all dressed in red, who hadn't stolen Snorri, but had somehow got hold of another pony like him.

'Hullo,' the boy said. 'My name is Leif. What's yours?'

'Mother,' Mordec said. 'Leif is a lost boy. We must find his parents. Until we do, we must look after him.'

'Of course,' Estrid says. 'Will you come with me, Leif? I am Estrid, mother of Mordec and Eyrin. Our home will be your home until we find your father and mother.'

Leif dismounted. 'What must I call you?' he asked.

'You can call me Estrid.'

'Can't I call you Mother, like Mordec does?'

'You can,' Estrid said. 'Or even Mama like Eyrin does.'

'I think I called someone Mama,' Leif said. 'I'll call you Mother. And I want you to know that I showed Mordec the way when he couldn't see.'

'He did that. Sometimes down a blind path, but we'll forget that. He got us both to a safe place and me to a pair of glasses,' Mordec said, laughing. 'We'll tell you all about it.'

'And now you've brought him safely home to me,' Estrid said to Leif. Upon which Leif put his arms round her and hugged her. Estrid kissed him on his forehead. 'You are most welcome,' she said.

'She's NOT your mother,' Eyrin said, pulling him away.

'All right then, you tell me what I can call her,' Leif said, folding his arms and looking down challengingly at Eyrin's frowning face.

'You can call her Eyrin's mother.'

'It's a deal,' Leif said. 'Now let me show you something I've brought specially for you.'

'What is it?'

'Come and see,' Leif said, leading him to where the packhorses had begun to graze on the side of the road.

'Where's Father?' Mordec asked Estrid, peering about the orchard and straining to look into the distance. 'Shall I shout for him?'

'He's not here. Not yet.'

'Not yet? Where's he gone? Will he be home soon?'

'Yes. He'll be home soon. Come inside, and we can tell each other everything. Leave the boys. I want to hear all you have to tell me.'

Estrid led the way into the house, clutching his hand tightly. But Mordec insisted on being told where Hauk was before he would begin to relate his own long story.

'Gone looking for me? On Bjarwulf's ship? Then he must have set out before he got my messages that I was safe.'

'We got no messages that you were safe. Not before or after he set out.'

'I sent pigeons,' Mordec said. 'To Julius the Troll. I thought he would send the messages on to you. Why didn't he? What happened?'

'I don't believe Julius the Troll himself could have got your messages. He would have sent then on to us for sure. As soon as he got Hauk's message that you were safe he let us know that very day.'

'Father's message that I was safe? From where?'

'From a place called Runnydale, on the far side of England, in the country of the Celts called Wales. Olaf the Shipbuilder says he had been to Wales, though he does not know this place called Runnydale—'

'Runnydale? But that was where I was. That's where I sent my messages from. So Father traced me to Runnydale! How did he do that, I wonder. It must have been Zarath who sent the pigeons with his messages. Yet he wouldn't do it for me. I had to steal two of his pigeons … What else did his messages say?'

'That he was starting home. That he'd be here in a few days.'

'How many days ago?'

'Four. He will be here any day now.'

'Bjarwulf's ship is sturdy and fast—and if he doesn't pause to raid another on the way …'

He was interrupted by a blast on a trumpet, followed by several more blasts, getting louder as the trumpeter came nearer the house. Eyrin appeared in the door, the brightly shining trumpet at his lips, with Leif close behind him.

'Look what the red boy has given me, Mama,' Eyrin said, and blew another ear-splitting blast.

Estrid and Mordec put their hands over their ears.

'That's wonderful,' Estrid said. 'Now take it to the meadow and never blow it in the house again—please!'

Mordec told the tale of his adventures over supper that evening, leaving out most of the details. He knew he would have to tell it many times more.

Estrid asked many questions about her father. Was he in good health? Where was the moveable Blue City now? Was his business doing well? Was his servant Clavi, Keeper of the Keys, still with him? …

Mordec answered her questions, which came tumbling over each other. At last she paused, and he told her, 'Grandfather sent you some books and a gold necklace, but they were lost with all my things. Maybe Bjarwulf has them. I'll ask him when he gets back.'

'We know that Hengist and Horsa remained with Father,' Estrid said. 'Gus brought letters from them to their folks.'

'Oh, I know about the letters,' Mordec said with a laugh. 'I wrote them.'

Eyrin and Leif fell asleep before Mordec had begun to tell the part about the voyage from Genova to Sam's island. Estrid roused Leif enough to have him walk sleepily to a bed, and carried Eyrin to another. She covered them with furs and kissed them both on the top of their dreaming heads.

When the firelight was burning low, and the night was so shrill with crickets that it seemed the noise and silence were the same thing, Mordec asked his mother where was Gus son of Hakon.

'Mordec, Gus is with your father. He begged to go with him on the search for you.'

'Then you know what happened?'

Estrid nodded.

'What did Gus say?'

'He said—he said he shut you in—on the—' Estrid's voice choked on the words, 'the burning ship.'

'He did? He said he did? He confessed it?'

She nodded, trying to see the look in his eyes by the dim red light of the dying fire, but all she saw was the red glow reflected in his glasses.

'So it *was* Gus.' Mordec said quietly. 'I thought it might be. I—I was afraid it might be.'

'You did not know? You were not sure who it was?'

'No.'

They stared into the embers for a long moment, then both started speaking at once—'He's ashamed'—Estrid began.

'I didn't want to believe—' Mordec began.

They both fell silent again for another long moment.

'It will be for you to decide his punishment, of course,' Estrid said quietly. 'No one will tell you what you should do. He knows that.'

'Did he … did he say *why*?' Mordec asked.

Estrid shook her head. 'Don't *you* have some idea …?'

'None. I'll want him to tell me why before I can decide anything. I can't think of anything I did to hurt him.'

Mordec rose suddenly and paced the floor, and cried out passionately, 'Now he knows that I survived—they would've been told in Runnydale that I was found alive—once he knew that—now that he knows it—*he* should decide his punishment. He should not wait for me to decide it. Let him give up his own life. He should plunge into the waves. He should not be coming home.'

Estrid put a finger to her lips. 'Sh-shh,' she said, though whether to calm his anger or to stop him waking the boys, she herself was not sure. She was deeply disturbed by the pain in Mordec's voice. Though she could not see the look on his face, she could hear that he was torn, and understood how hard it was for him to bear the certain knowledge that his friend had tried to murder him—and in so cruel a manner—and that he now bore, alone, the terrible burden of judgment.

mostly happy, partly true

On each of the next four days, Mordec went soon after dawn to sit on the edge of the highest cliff in the range that rose sheer out of the sea. He'd stay there, peering through his glasses into the west for the sight of a sail, until the sun was overhead.

Then he would go to help Estrid in their orchard and sheds. But again every evening, when the work was done and he'd eaten supper at a table in the orchard with Estrid and Eyrin and Leif, he returned to his look-out place, leaving it only when the light of the lengthening days became too dim for him to see the horizon, and almost too dim for him to see his way home.

Their daily work was often interrupted by friends and neighbours, calling in to welcome Mordec home, and to ask for his story. To all of them he'd say, 'I'll tell you everything when my father is back. He must hear it first.'

Some boys discovered that Leif was only too happy to tell them his story about the night Mordec was 'magicked' by the great magician Zarath of the East to suddenly appear in the great hall of the palace of Runnydale and be the very Viking friend he had asked for. He would have told them much more—about their climb over the mountain, their long walk, their amazing adventures in Owaindale—but Mordec had sternly ordered him to say nothing about any of that under threat of many and dire (though undescribed) penalties if he dared to disobey.

'Can't I even tell Eyrin's mother about the Princess who came to Runnydale very fat and then became quite thin?'

'Yes. You can tell Eyrin's mother anything if she can bear listening to your endless chatter. She knows everything anyway, and she won't tell anyone else. Not until I've told my father all that happened to me. Until then, you must keep our secret.'

'I will, Mordec. I promise. You know I won't say anything if you tell me not to, I never did—did I?'

'True. You never did and you won't now. Until I say you can. Understood?'

'Understood. Can't I even tell Eyrin about going to school in Runnydale?'

'Yes. You can tell him about going to school.'

'I could teach him Welsh. He likes to sit on his pony and blow his trumpet while I sit on mine and lead him round the meadow. I'd rather teach him Welsh. Though I don't know a lot of it.'

'You could do that. If he wants to learn it.'

'Will I go to school here?'

'We don't have a school. We should. It's a good idea. But don't worry, my mother will teach you. She taught me. And we have quite a lot of books.'

In the afternoon of the fourth day, when only some boys playing on the beach were there to see it, Bjarwulf's ship with its great square sail loomed black against the burning sky.

The boys ran to spread the news. One shouted to Mordec over the gate of the orchard, 'Bjarwulf's back!', and Mordec and Estrid stopped what they were doing. Estrid picked up Eyrin, Leif came running to catch up with Mordec, and they soon stood among a crowd gathered to greet the Serpent King as its crew rowed the famous ship over the yellow path of the sea, past the breakwater, and into the still water of the harbour.

There was Captain Bjarwulf himself, and Pelf, and Delfinola, and—greeted by a loud cheer as he stepped ashore—Hauk the Meadmaker, father of Mordec.

Father and son embraced, laughing with happiness. Then Hauk embraced Estrid, and took Eyrin from her arms and held him high, and they all laughed with happiness, Eyrin the longest. He was not sure why there was so much laughter, but he enjoyed it.

'And this,' Hauk said, when he'd put Eyrin down and noticed a boy standing back but watching them, 'is Leif?'

'Yes,' Eyrin said as Leif nodded. 'His name's Leif, and he has a pony just like mine.'

Hauk put his hands on the boy's shoulders.

'I'm glad to meet you, Leif. Slate told me about you when I was in Runnydale. And Zarath told me that you wished for a friend, and so he gave you Mordec.'

'They told you? I wanted to tell you myself.'

'I'd much rather hear about it from you.'

'Now that you're home Mordec will let me tell everybody everything,' Leif said. 'So I'm really glad you're here.'

While this was happening, Mordec was looking among the crew coming off the ship for Gus. He wanted to see him but not be seen by him. But Hakon and Gus had disembarked while Mordec was greeting Hauk, and had slipped quietly away behind the backs of the crowd. Hakon's wife Tove—a big woman with yellow hair hanging in a thick braid—joined them, took Gus's hand in her own without a word, and led them to where two men stood in armour with their swords drawn.

'Go with them bravely, son,' Hakon said to Gus. 'You have no choice.'

Gus nodded. He embraced his mother, who had tears on her full round cheeks, and let the armed men march him away—each of them clasping one of his arms firmly above the elbow—to the jail behind the hall of the Thing. It was a large circular room, lined with benches, lit by barred windows. A jailor locked him in, the only prisoner.

Hakon and Tove went home and said little to each other. They did not join the crowds who went to Hauk's house and Bjarwulf's warehouse to hear their stories. Many of the listeners groaned every time they heard how one night the seekers and the sought passed each other on the sea.

For laughter they asked again and again for the story of how Mordec and the others had gone to Italy to rescue Lily's mother from captivity, thinking she was held against her will by a Viking warrior, but had found her happily married to him.

'So he'd captured not *her* but her heart,' one of the wives explained when she told the story to another wife.

The women asked Delfinola many questions about the dinner party at the house of Slate in Runnydale, the food on his table, the clothes and jewels the Princess Starling wore; and, over and over again, they asked Mordec about the court of Owaindale, the customs, the clothes, the dances.

The men too enjoyed hearing how Mordec, mistaken for a lost Prince, ruled for a time over that land. It made them proud.

But the men were most interested in the events at the Abbey of the Black Monks; how Mordec had called upon Thor to save Gus son of Hakon from death, and the god had used Mordec's arm to drop his hammer on a Black Monk who was in the act of striking Gus a killing blow with an axe. They were interested for two reasons. First, because the story would be a part of the case when they sat as judges in Gus's trial before the Thing. And also because they had heard that an army of Christians was being formed to force the people of the north to become Christians too.

There was one detail of his adventures that Mordec did not talk about. They knew he had been locked in the hold of a burning ship, and he often described how he had forced his way out with more strength than he knew he possessed. But he said nothing about who had locked him in. No one expected him to. Gus son of Hakon had confessed. Not one of them—no man, no woman—spoke Gus's name to Mordec. By mutual consent, guided by custom, all would keep silent on the matter of the crime and the criminal until he was brought before the Thing and Mordec himself declared his punishment.

From Bjarwulf the men liked most to hear how he had passed between the islands of Orkney and Zetland, in whose harbours a multitude of Viking ships were moored, and the raiders liked to come aboard each others' vessels to look in their holds and wonder—both admiringly and jealously—at others' hoards of loot. They could not hear it often enough repeated that Bjarwulf had passed among them without stopping because he had a hold empty of any goods except a few hams, harps and trumpets, some of which he had bought, and some he had received *as a gift*.

He told how he had protested that he did not want to take the route between the islands because he had nothing in his hold, but how Hauk had pleaded with him not to go south and then up the east coast of England because it would take them longer to get home. It was Delfinola wife of Pelf, he said, who had settled the dispute. And at that point in the telling, Delfinola herself would often rise and recite her argument.

'Captain,' she would say, reenacting the scene and addressing Bjarwulf as she had that night off the coast of Runnydale, 'our hold is full of gold. We are in a great hurry to get it safely home. It is the largest and the most precious hoard ever you have won in all your famous voyages on all the seas of the wild world. No—do not say it is not so. Do not remind me that we have an almost empty hold. I say it is full of gold, and all the other Vikings, all the pirates and all the traders will believe it too. And their hearts will be wrung with jealousy. How will we get them to believe it? By telling them, Captain. By telling them in song.'

And truly Delfinola had made up a grand song about that non-existent hoard of gold. They had sung it, she and all the ship's crew, and the passengers, and even Pelf her husband, as they passed each harbour of the islands, and every Viking ship.

Delfinola related: 'Oh yes! Every moored or moving ship. Under the eyes of the other pirates, we were more boastful than ever they were, more hurried, more thrilled, more loud, as though we were drunk with victory. And how we laughed, and shouted, and sang, all waving our arms in the air. They saw never a glint of gold, but only our white teeth as we laughed our way between the isles, among their ships, making a legend of our own, the ship that bore the golden hoard back to our home among the fjords.'

The men cheered and cried out, 'Sing it, Lady Delfinola, sing it for us.'

Then she would have Bjarwulf and Pelf, Lars and whoever else of Bjarwulf's men were there, line up ready to join in the chorus; with flagons in their hands to wave about and wet their throats; and ready

to stamp and jump and make a great show of celebrating the raids they had not made and the plunder
they had not got.

Delfinola would stand and sing in her lovely voice:

Oh, the moon is made of silver
And the stars are made of tin
And dawn's a copper curtain
That lets the daylight in.

Then she would lift her arms and the chorus would
ring out:

What's in my hold?
What's in my hold?
Hams and a harp
Trumpets and tin
AND SILVER AND COPPER
AND GOLD GOLD GOLD.

All the men would stand up to repeat the chorus
and cheer.

'It is partly true,' Delfinola said to Estrid when she
took her a Runnydale ham, and Mordec's books from
The Good Ship Good. 'Hams and a harp, trumpets
and tin, those we truly did have, dear heart. And isn't
"partly true" the best that can be said for every song
that ever was sung?'

Estrid did not deny it. Besides, she was distracted
by the gold necklace Delfinola was wearing, wondering whether she dared to ask: 'Was that necklace

found on The Good Ship Good, because I think it is the one my father sent me.' But she did not ask. After all, she couldn't be sure.

One night after Leif and Eyrin had been tucked into bed and kissed good-night by Estrid, and Eyrin had fallen asleep, Hauk came and sat beside Leif and said: 'I have something to show you.'

He held out his hand on which lay the small silver chain-bracelet with the name 'Leif' engraved on one long solid link. He had mended its broken clasp.

'See there it has your name on it. Is it yours? Do you remember if you ever wore it?'

Leif took it and gazed at it wonderingly. 'I did have one like this when I was small. I remember mine had two humps on the back of it and some gold spots.'

He took it from Hauk and turned the long link over. 'Yes! Look. There are the humps. And there are the spots of gold. It *is* mine. Where did you find it? Somewhere near here? Does it mean that my father and mother live somewhere near here? Do you know them? Will they come for me?'

'We don't know them but we will find them,' Hauk said. 'Let me fasten it on your arm. It brought me luck. It will bring you luck too.'

saga of a hero

A different song was sung in the mead hall on the glorious night when all came together to celebrate the successes of Mordec's quest and what would become the legendary search for him when he was lost.

All the Vikings who could get to Hauk's mead hall within a day's journey were there (except Hakon the Tanner). Hauk did a roaring trade. Mordec sat a little apart from the rest, by now quite used to being the centre of attention, but expecting to enjoy it as much as ever.

The Skald, tall and flat, a little stooped, his white robe hanging from his frail shoulders to his shoes, belted with bronze medallions linked with loops of gold, was seated on a chair with a new harp beside him. His white hair framed his long, fine-boned face and fell in tangled locks over his shoulders, and his sparse beard twisted down is chest. His blind eyes looked as if they were made of pale blue glass. On a barrel beside him stood a flagon of ale, a horn of beer, and a glass of mead. When the hall fell silent and his moment arrived, he felt for each vessel in turn, the flagon, the horn, the glass, and swallowed a mouthful from each of them.

He struck a chord on his harp. But he was not intending to sing. Tonight he was to recite a saga. The strings of the harp he would pluck only now and then, for dramatic effect.

He began:

With a Queen, a Queen's daughter,
To find the Queen's mother
Captured by Vikings,
Our Viking to save one
Whom Vikings had captured,

Daring danger he quested,
Wandered far, fearless,
Swimming wide rivers
Riding wave-horses
On ships of strangers
To search foreign lands.

Daring danger he quested,
With friends, fellow Vikings,
Far wandering fearless
With a Queen, a Queen's daughter,
To find the Queen's mother
Captured by Vikings.

They came to an Island
Where Sam the Magician
Though crossed by Christians
Yet worked his wonders
And he mapped the way
To find the lost Queen.

Daring danger they quested
And came upon Vikings
Alive in disgrace
After losing in battle,
And ever in fear
Of a dark dwarfish foe.

Four men with few weapons,
Our Vikings defeated
The dark dwarfish foe.
But the men of disgrace
Gave them no thanks,
Only plotted to kill them.

Faithless as ever
They plotted to kill them.
The four were outnumbered
Though the young Queen
Fought with them.
Their doom seemed certain
But fearless they faced it.

Then they bethought them
Of a ruse fit for legend,
To roll rough rocks
Down on the cowards.
And so they lived, victors,
The men and the Queen.

Then on they quested
With the Queen, a Queen's daughter,
To find the Queen's mother
Captured by Vikings.

Our Viking to save one
Whom Vikings had captured.

The Queen, the Queen's daughter
Was captured by strangers
Bound and restrained
By a Cailiph's rich daughter.
But our four redeemed her
And bore her to safety.

For a season they lingered
In the town of the Lombards
The town that floats
Where fair weather takes it.
A town where an old man is kin
To our Viking.
AIn procession with Christians
They pressed on, proceeded,
To the town where wayfarers
Told them the Queen was,
The Queen that they sought,
Queen's mother, Queen's daughter.

There they found
The Queen's mother,
Queen of the Fenreach,
Not fettered in bondage
Not bound but free,
And esteemed in her town.

The Queen of the Fenreach
Was wife to a Viking,
Rorick his name.

She gifted her Queendom
To her brave daughter.
So ended the quest
Of our four Vikings.

Two Vikings lingered
In the land of the Lombards,
And two set sail
With the Queen of the Fenreach,
On the ship of a woman
Anwid her name,
Bearing cargo to England.

They paused at the island
Of Sam the Magician,
And found that the Christians
Who lived on the island
Were plotting to slaughter
Sam the Magician.

Sam the Magician
Must contend with the Abbott,
The chief of the Christians
Not with swords, not with words,
But with magic merely
To save his own life.

Three days they contested
Each working his magic,
Each weaving his spells,
Each working his wonders,
Three days in contest,
Magician and Abbott.

The cold Christian Abbot
Weaving his spells
With fire and birds,
Dances and Christian
Incantations,
To wither and waste
Sam the Magician.

Sam the Magician
Red-headed and warm,
Working his wonders
With water and passes
Signed to the sky.
He was more powerful.

Sam the Magician,
Red-headed, more powerful,
Changed the cold Abbot
And two of his brothers
Into dogs, whimpering.
Sam won the contest.

In vengeance a Christian
Lured one of our Vikings
Into their Godhouse
Plotting to kill him.
Plotting to cleave his skull
Through with an axe.

But our Viking, watching,
Called upon Thor,

And on the instant
Between the axe raised

And the axe falling,
Thor dropped his hammer
Down on the Christian,
Felled him with one blow
Down on the stone ground
Smashed and bleeding
Fallen and dying,
Soon dead as stone.

Although it was 'not done' to interrupt a recitation of a saga, applause broke out in the mead hall, and cheers, and Mordec smiled, reddened a little, and bowed his head.

The Skald frowned, and before the applause had quite died down, he plucked two strings of the harp, and resumed:

Then again on the waves
Our Vikings were borne
Onward for England
Blithe on the good ship
Bearing our men
And the Queen among women.

And sailing towards them
Stealthy in darkness
Came Bjarwulf the Viking,
King among Pirates,
Master and Captain of
The famed Serpent King,
Lord of the seas.

Another cheer went up, and Bjarwulf stood and punched a fist in the air.

The Skald drank deep from all the three vessels beside him, and was still drinking when silence fell. He cleared his throat, swept a hand over the strings of the harp, and went on:

No trove of treasure
Did Bjarwulf find
On the good ship.
But he took the cargo
Poor though it was,
And the crew, all women.
Then Bjarwulf's men
Upon his orders
Set fire to the good ship.
It burnt on the waters,
Enflaming the night.
Burning, it drifted.

Bjarwulf landed the Captain
Of the good ship
On England's shore.
And with her the Queen.
Then they sailed home.
All but one.

Our Viking was doomed,
Sealed in behind doors
Barricaded with barrels,
Trapped on the good ship
Burning and drifting,
As if destined to die.

He who had called to Thor,
And saved his companion
Was trapped on the good ship
Drifting and burning.
Who had condemned him
So direly to die?

Our Viking broke free
With his brawn and his boldness,
Found the ship drifting
No longer in flames.
Storm waves and tempest
Safe brought him to land.

'Twas the world of the Welshmen
Where our Viking landed.
They welcomed our Viking
And made him their ruler.
They clad him in blue
And they crowned him with gold.

They claimed him their ruler
And weighed him with gold,
With chains of pure gold
They held him in thrall.
A prisoner prince
Unheard of in saga.

Justly he judged them
And gently he won them
Until they so loved him

They sadly unbound him
And let him go home,

MORDEC THE HERO.
Daring he quested,
But he came home,
Laden with gold
Prince of the Welshmen,
Viking forever
MORDEC THE HERO.

The Skald's words were becoming a little slurred. But he raised his voice and went on:

MORDEC THE HERO,
MORDED THE HERO,
Prince of the Welshmen,
Daring he quested,
Came home laden
With gold, our hero …

His voice faded:

Mordec the Viking,
Mordec our hero …

The Skald slept and snored, one hand tangled in the harp strings.

Mordec was still blushing—something he had not expected would happen—and he looked at the floor when the silence fell. He continued to look down and continued to feel the heat of his face as the men left, many of them touching him on the shoulder in passing. Happy, uplifted in spirit, they emerged from the warm flame-lighted mead hall into the cool starry night.

The Skald was to complete and improve his saga and sing it in many a mead hall until it became famous. It was eventually written down, which is why we have it now. It includes the story of the search for Mordec. The names of Hengist and Horsa, Queen Lily, Bjarwulf and Hauk recur many times. And in a section that must have been added after the Thing heard the case against Gus son of Hakon, he is named and his treachery recorded, as is the punishment that Mordec pronounced upon him.

But it does not include Delfinola's songs, which the Skald considered vulgar.

mordec's revenge

The days before the day of judgment when the men would assemble in the Thingstead and rule on the guilt of wrong-doers and let the victims decide on their punishment were as few as only the fingers of one hand were needed to count, and still Mordec gave no sign to anyone—even when one or another of his friends raised the question with him—that he had made up his mind on Gus's punishment. He gave no answer, changed the subject.

Estrid, however, knew her son was brooding on the matter. He was absent-minded, often did not hear when she spoke to him.

He would let Leif tell him whopping fibs about what he had seen and done without laughing to show both his disbelief and his enjoyment of them. 'Oh, did you?' he would say seriously, or 'I see.' And Leif would go away disappointed.

When Eyrin asked him to hold him on his pony for a ride round the meadow, he would do it, but as though his thoughts were on something else.

More silent than usual, dressed daily in his old dark blue working clothes, he helped his father with the gathering of the honey, the boiling of the mead, the sealing and storing of the barrels. Hauk was pleased to see that his son's head had not been turned; that neither the praise of him being sung far and wide through the land, nor the riches he had brought home with him, had affected his character.

Hauk knew what was on Mordec's mind. He understood why he was not laughing. Had Mordec asked him for his advice he would not have been able or willing to give it. Only Mordec could know what he felt about Gus, what feelings about each other had been built through their shared perils.

Hauk did not tell Mordec how Gus had shown every sign of deep regret. He did not tell him that Gus had wept with relief when he knew for sure that Mordec had survived the burning ship. He waited to see what Mordec would choose; whether he would exact the extreme vengeance the law allowed him; or was weighing *this* up against *that* to try to be just; or would relent to emotion and grant mercy.

As for Gus, the days went by all too fast as what he thought of as his doom approached. His rightful doom, he called it to himself. Rightful, whatever it might be. He forced himself to think of it being the worst—a lifetime of thralldom for him, as well as his family losing everything, selling all they possessed to pay the compensation, the Wergeld, to the erstwhile friend he had tried to kill.

Though the days passed too quickly for him, yet the hours were slow. Locked in the big round stone room behind the Thingstead, the only prisoner, he had little to occupy him but thoughts of his ruined future. Sometimes one of his guards would play a game of hnefatafl with him, and when they had finished—the guard almost always winning—would leave the board and pieces on the wooden bench that ran round the room and was Gus's bed, seat, and table, in case Gus wanted to play the game against himself.

Through barred windows Gus could see the edge of green cliffs in the distance, and beyond that a strip of the sea. Would he ever go to sea again? Perhaps he would—as Mordec's bondsman. As man and bondsman the two of them would grow old together. His life would be what Mordec made it. But whatever he might have to do, he would be forever in thrall, forever poor, without pride, without honour. He would have no wife …

A picture of Lily rose in his imagination, only to be quickly dismissed. If ever he saw her again, it would likely be because she was Mordec's wife.

At such moments he would pull the hnefatafl board towards him and concentrate on arranging the pieces. Or walk about the room and force himself to think of other things.

But there was one thing that the thought of Lily gave rise to which offered him hope.

War! There was almost certainly to be war between the Vikings and the English. It would be so big a war that every man who could fight would be brought on to the field. Every man who could fight would be needed. Even bondsmen and thralls, even prisoners, would be drafted into the army of the Vikings. True, as a bondsman he would have to serve under the command of his master Mordec, but at least he would get to fight. That was the future he had been born for. He could yet win honour as a warrior even if he was a thrall. And if he died in battle, whether as free man or bondsman, he would go to Valhalla.

With such thoughts his spirits rose. And for a moment he could think of Lily again without striving to turn the thought off, because it was not about marriage but battle, how he and Lily had spoken of single combat with each other.

But, 'No!' he commanded himself. 'Do not think of her at all. Think of standing before the judges. Think of the strength you will need to become a bondsman instead of a free man, a servant instead of a warrior. Because there may not be a war. So prepare yourself!'

On the day before the Thing was due to start its sitting, he had dozed off after trying to play a game of hanefatafl against himself. The sun had started on its descent, and was pouring its light and warmth into the prison through the barred windows. A bee had made its way in between the bars and was buzzing about trying to find its way out. Hot and drowsy, Gus's head fell on his chest as he leant back against the stone wall.

Something woke him—it might have been the sound of the prison door being unlocked, opened, closed, and locked again. But trying to hold on to a dream he was having, he was reluctant to open his eyes. When he did he saw that someone dressed in dark blue was standing in the middle of the room looking intently at him through a pair of glasses, with arms folded and booted feet planted apart. The boots, which were very handsome, as glossy a brown as freshly peeled chestnuts, were not familiar. But there was only one Viking who wore glasses.

'Mordec!'

The name burst out, but hoarsely. Gus cleared his throat, half rose, but sank back again.

For a few moments the two looked into each other's eyes from a distance in silence. Then Gus, still seated on the bench, dropped his gaze, leant forward, hung his arms limply between his knees, and bowed his head.

It was he who spoke first.

'I'm not going to plead with you, Mordec. Whatever you decide I will accept without complaining. I know what I deserve.'

'What do you deserve' Mordec asked quietly. 'For doing what?'

'You know what.'

'I want to hear it from you.'

'For … locking you in the ship's hold. For … trying to kill you.'

'And what should be your punishment for that?'

'Wergeld?'

Mordec made no answer.

'Being your bondsman?'

No answer.

'Both?'

'Your bondsman for … ten years?'

Still no answer.

'Twenty?'

Mordec kept his silence.

Gus's next question came very quietly.

'For … life?'

Still Mordec said nothing. He walked slowly to the bench and moved a piece on the hnefatafl board.

Gus watched him anxiously. His silence was ominous. What did he intend? Something even worse? Would Mordec sell him into foreign slavery? Perhaps to the Moors or the tin-miners?

At last Mordec spoke.

'There is one thing I want to know,' he said, moving another piece on the board.

'What?' Gus said.

Mordec dropped his hand to his side, straightened up, and looking at Gus again he said, '*Why?*'

Gus shook his head as if he didn't understand.

'Why, Gus? Why did you try to kill me?'

'You don't know?'

'I don't know.'

'Didn't you know that I was jealous of you?'

'Jealous of me for what reason?'

'Because of Lily.'

'Because of Lily? Lily didn't care for me. She was in love with you.'

'But you and she … You seemed to understand each other. And she was so desperate to save you from being executed. I'll tell you this—I rode like Thor on his lightning bolt to help you for *her* sake more than for yours.'

Mordec's voice was quiet when he answered the question Gus had not asked but which hung in the air between them.

'If you're asking me was I drawn to Lily, the answer is yes, I was. Of course I was. But she was not drawn to me. Not in that way. Yes, she was desperate to save me, and yes, that was—partly—because she liked me. But she also wanted me to live so I could do something for her. You know what it was. To go and parley with Ingolf to let her mother go. Why did she think I was the man to do it? Hmm. I think it has something to do with the eyeglasses. They make me look wise.'

'Are you joking?'

'Only a little.'

'You two—you were always laughing together.'

'Yes, but everyone except you could see she was in love with you. All her talk about fighting you was a way of saying how strongly she felt. Delfinola told you that with her song about two lovers killing each other as they kissed.'

'Tell me truly, Mordec—some of those times you were laughing with Lily, weren't you *trying* to make me jealous?'

'Perhaps I was. I might have been. I wanted to tease you, yes, with your lost look whenever I made a joke.'

'I thought you were laughing at me. Both of you. Then I thought, if you weren't there …'

'And how did that work out? Did she come home with you? Is she here, is she your bride?'

'No. As far as I know she is home in England—preparing to make war on us.'

Mordec went to the window. Looking out of it at the sunset, he said thoughtfully, 'It's true that the English are preparing for war with us. We are preparing for it too. The warlord Tostig son of Tostig is gathering the greatest Viking army ever assembled. Armour for men and horses is being beaten into shape in every town. Boys as young as twelve are being drilled for battle. New ships are being built, whole forests of tall larches felled for the mainmasts. It won't be long before the gods will watch as the sea between here and England becomes the rocking floor of wooden bottoms so crammed with warriors the oars will have to be held upright when they aren't being plied, because there'll be no space for them inside the ships.'

'Tostig son of Tostig? Commander Tostig! He is to lead the army? Then we will certainly win!'

'We will win,' Mordec echoed, 'with the help of Thor.'

At the mention of Thor, Gus again dropped his head. Instantly he remembered how Thor's hammer had fallen on the monk who was about to kill him—from the hand of Mordec.

'Can I know? Will you tell me before the Thing begins tomorrow?' he asked.

'Tell you what penalty I will demand?'

'Yes. Will you tell me now? Am I to be your bondsman?'

'No,' Mordec replied. He walked slowly round the room; stopped to watch the setting sun through the barred western windows. 'No,' he said again. 'I do not want a bondsman.'

'Wergeld? My father will sell all we have. We will go as beggars …'

'No', Mordec said, walking on slowly. 'No, I do not want Wergeld.'

'Then … what?'

'I will ask,' Mordec said, stopping near Gus and speaking thoughtfully, 'that they leave you behind when the army sails for England. That you alone of all the Vikings in the world be left at home.'

He spoke casually, and strolled on again.

Gus rose to his feet, drew himself up to his full height and advanced a few slow paces. He was an inch or so taller than Mordec. The setting sun made his hair glow like gold, and the shadow of a bar fell down the middle of his face.

'No-o!' he cried out. 'No, Mordec, please. I—I know I said I would not plead with you but now I am pleading. Don't do that to me. That is the worst punishment you could impose on me. You know that. Don't do it. I'll serve you. All my life. After the battle. But I must fight. It was what I was born for. You know that I am a warrior born, Mordec. And—and our folk need me. They need my skills. I must go with the army. I must!'

Mordec smiled.

'Yes. You are a warrior born, as you say. So that is what I will ask the Thing to rule. That you are forbidden to join Tostig's army.'

Gus returned to the bench and sat down slowly.

'Won't you bring a sword and kill me instead? You have taken away my reason to live.'

'You asked me. I've told you,' Mordec said.

'The worst,' Gus said, 'The very worst you could do to me.'

He choked on the last words. He felt anger rise in him. He clenched his fists, and only with an effort restrained himself from rushing at his judge and letting them speak for him. Instead, he threw back his head, gritted his teeth and squeezed his eyes shut.

Mordec turned away and made for the door. He raised his hand to knock the signal to the jailer to come and let him out, but his hand paused in the air.

'Do you remember,' he said cheerfully, 'the White Knight, Sir Baz? The White Knight who turned out to be black when he raised his visor after the joust in England? In the Earldom of Linkard? Strange, but I have a sudden memory of him. A lone knight, wandering freely where he will, fighting the fights he chooses to fight, beholden to no man. Now I wonder why he suddenly comes to my mind. Because we were speaking of England, I suppose, and fighting. Well, I'll say goodnight to you. See you tomorrow at the Thing.'

Gus made no reply. He heard the door open and close again, the key turn in the lock.

He drooped his head in despair and sat still as the room darkened, as the sun sank into the sea. For an hour or more he did not move and tried not to think.

But when he he looked up and saw only the stars through the window, he thought, 'Out there in the west is England, where a war will be fought.' And Mordec's words came back to him. 'Where a lone knight wanders free, fighting the fights he chooses to fight, beholden to no man …'

And suddenly he smiled.

He rose in the dark, went to the window, breathed in the cool night air, stood tall, felt his strength.

A burst of laughter broke from him at last. He saw the joke!

'Mordec!' he murmured. 'You sly rogue. You are setting me free!'